SIMON, FRIENDS, AND THE DREAM STEALER

Book One

by
R. E. Brémaud

Order this book online at www.trafford.com
or email orders@trafford.com

Most Trafford titles are also available at major online book retailers.

Printed in the United States of America.

ISBN: 978-1-4269-4551-9 (sc)
ISBN: 978-1-4269-4552-6 (hc)
ISBN: 978-1-4269-4553-3 (e)

Library of Congress Control Number: 2010915627

Trafford rev. 11/03/2010

 www.trafford.com

North America & international
toll-free: 1 888 232 4444 (USA & Canada)
phone: 250 383 6864 ♦ fax: 812 355 4082

Contents

Acknowledgments   vii

Prologue   ix

Chapter One – Dreamville   1

Chapter Two – Principal Toombs Confiscates Simon's Dreams   10

Chapter Three – Principal Toombs Scheme   19

Chapter Four – Interrupted Summer Festival   31

Chapter Five – The Ancient Doctrine of Dreamville   41

Chapter Six – Simon's On Trial   49

Chapter Seven – Everything's Seemingly Back to Normal   57

Chapter Eight – Opening Night   66

Chapter Nine – Dreamvillians Are Stunned   76

Chapter Ten – Chaos in Dreamville   85

Chapter Eleven – Fugitives   95

Chapter Twelve – The Escapees   104

Chapter Thirteen- Rino Has Difficulty Presenting His Evidence   114

Chapter Fourteen – Simon Reveals the Truth   122

Chapter Fifteen – Fairytale Monday   133

Epilogue   137

<u>Acknowledgments</u>

I'd like to thank anyone and everyone who believes in this project and simply enjoys imaginative fiction and understands the value of dreams coming true.

I have a great amount of gratitude for the entire talented publishing team at Trafford for their time and energy spent on making my books a reality for me, my being published is my dream come true.

I dedicate this book to all who believe in making their dreams a reality, to my friends out there and my deceased mother who passed away in my opinion too soon.

<u>Prologue</u>

Dreamville Hospital
6:02 A.M.

Mr. and Mrs. Dreamlee are in their hospital room dreamily enjoying the sight of their first child. They anxiously wait to know what they will name their newborn bouncing baby boy when Grandpa Dreamlee enters the hospital room with the news that the dreamy king's son has lost his mind and no one has any idea why. The whole hospital is resonating with the whispering of Dreamvillians regarding this terrible news but Mr. and Mrs. Dreamlee just smile with joy as one of the eldest Dreamvillian elders enters their hospital room. He is the next Dreamvillian king's father.

He approaches the Dreamlee baby boy and looks at his mother with a sparkle in his eyes he places his right hand on the baby boy's forehead and says, "Let the truth always be with you." A bright white light follows this amicable royal gesture and at that moment the elder sits in a spare chair by the bed and says, "The boy's name is Simon. He will be…" He barely says his name when he dies on the spare chair at the foot of the bed when a Dreamvillian man enters the room and is unrecognizable to anybody. He collects the eldest elder's body which is never to be heard of or spoken of again from that moment on.

From that day on and for the next twelve years and despite all the adjustment they and all Dreamvillians have had to make, the Dreamlee's wondered what their beloved musically inclined son Simon Dreamlee will be. What did the deceased Dreamvillian King Régimand DreamRoyal the ninth mean?

Chapter One – Dreamville

It's always summer in the unknown town of Dreamville. A small town found in the farthest point of the southern hemisphere. If you blink, you'll miss it but if you close your eyes and imagine a town inhabited by imaginative, creative, artistic, scientific, and musically inclined people dressed in colorful clothing then you're halfway there. Picture big white houses, surrounded by white picket fences, and adorning all the yards are bright and colorful lights. The green grass is not just green grass but well manicured yards with bushes in all shapes, colors and sizes. Picture every yard has a silvery water fountain with a miniature cascading water fall for the colorful birds. The children of all ages, height and ethnicity are all pink cheeked, healthy, happy and well behaved. They all play in the paved streets without worrying about being harmed or kidnapped. They all ride their red hover bikes up and down the designated and un-forbidden trails in the surrounding woods without fear of being attacked by the wild animals. The adults feed and take care of the wild animals as if they are their own house pets. Every household in Dreamville has a cat, a dog, a bird and a fish as pets. Every weekend, these Dreamvillians have never ending summer festivities each time the crops are harvested. They celebrate every growing season gone by with freshly picked apples made into apple pies topped with fresh whip cream, raspberry, strawberry and blueberry jams spread on crackers and breads, fresh salads made with greens straight from the community gardens, chocolate made from fresh coco and fresh squeezed orange juice from the orange trees. Of course, the meals change from one festival to the next. Afterwards, the musically inclined Dreamvillians all play music and sing. Every musically inclined child has an instrument they play well, even though they can play any and every instrument, plus, they can all sing with their angelic voices like angels. In this paradise, for the parents, parenting is easy and carefree when every child goes to bed when they're told. The children like going to sleep just to dream. Their dreams fill them with ideas and potential. Even though everyone dreams, no one ever has nightmares. If you can imagine this wonderful place then you automatically know that every one of the Dreamvillians in Dreamville are happy to live in this creative town whose economic wealth depends on each and every one of their dreams, especially, when they come true.

The most recent town map has many streets that all include the word Dream, in fact, all family names include the word dream as well. Dreamtrue School is located on DreamHappy Street. The Parliament buildings are located on DreamBig Drive just off of the Hoverway. The never needed Dreamville dream squad police station and prison is located on JustDream Boulevard. The Dreamville mall is located on DreamLight Street. However, the town has a lone hill where a very sinister presence resides, Principal Toombs. He lives in the most unusual house up on that only hill overlooking the town. He lives alone in a black house with a black fence. The windows are painted black to block out the light. The trees are overgrown and all dead. Mice and rats run freely in his yard of two meter high dead grass. Instead of water silvery fountains with cascading water features, charcoal grey statues of gargoyles decorate the yard. The ancient thick grape vines, plants, flowers and grass are overgrown and dead. No one dares talk to him unless they have no choice. He's a menacing, tall figure that none of the kids like. He's mean, loud, and scary. Instead of a classic, clean, flattering black suit, he's always dressed in the same dingy shabby faded un-kept and dirty black pants, shirt and suit jacket. His eyes are big, round and dark. He never smiles at the kids and he never encourages them. He laughs at them when they get bad grades and he doesn't congratulate them when they get good grades. His teeth are yellow like the whites of his eyes, his finger nails are dirty, his hairs white even though he's young at only forty years old and his nose is pointy. He's a very unappealing man. The townspeople and the parents of Dreamville have made many requests to have him removed from the school system but all attempts have failed. For the past ten years he's brought doom and gloom to the lives of the school children. He walks the corridors checking in on kids in the classrooms as he walks by them. Poking his head in the doorways of the classrooms like a turtle to try and catch the children who dare to misbehave. He never hides his disappointment when he doesn't catch any of them being bad. In this town everyone's neighbors and one little boy including his family have the misfortune of being this scary principal's closest neighbor.

On Dreamway Street, in the Deamlee's house, a red haired woman with red lipstick, dressed in a white suit adorned in images of strawberries, stands at the kitchen window covered with yellow curtains with pictures of butterflies. She hums as she takes out the dishes from her stainless steel dishwasher and puts it on the counter. She stops humming and says, "Simon dear, come and help mommy with the dishes!" Simon, twelve years old, is short for his age, brunette, blue eyed and likes to dress in plaids and stripes. Simon's in the attic gazing at the stars when he hears his mother calling him. He's gazing out of his telescope at the stars and says to himself, "Aha, right there, the constellation of O'Brian." He confirms his finding with the internet site he researched and says, "Yeah, that's what I saw alright." He shuts his hand held computer off and starts down the stairs and says, "Coming mom." He enters the kitchen and helps her put the dishes in the large drawers. His mother smiles at him like she always does and says, "We're done so now it's your bedtime dear." Simon looks at the drawn curtains and asks, "Mom, why do you never open those curtains?" Mrs. Dreamlee looks at her son and says, "Oh well, there's not a good view so I close the curtains. It's nothing for you to concern yourself with. Now go to bed. Sweet dreams." Simon says, "Sweet dreams mom." He goes up to his room on the second floor and straight to bed. Mr. Dreamlee, a quirky scientific man sticks his head in his son's room and says, "Sweet dreams son." Simon says, "Sweet dreams dad." His female black Labrador dog jumps on the edge of the bed and lies down to sleep. Simon says, "Sweet dreams Boomboom Booya." Simon attaches the dream catcher to his head and falls asleep as soon as his head touches his pillow. Instantaneously, Simon begins to dream.

Being a musically inclined dreamer, Simon dreams about music notes. Throughout the course of his dream, these simple music notes fade into sheet music. This sheet music turns into a vivid lyrical piece of a musical. Simon can vividly hear the music in his brain while he dreams. He can even see the notes dancing off of the sheet music that lead him to the story behind his music. The music fades into the image of two dancers on a stage portraying the love of two people, a man and a woman, being destroyed by a third dancer portraying another woman who loves the man but he does not love her. Out of a fit of jealousy, this woman decides that if she can't have him than no one can and breaks the couple up making the man miserable for the rest of his life. What's not clear in Simon's dream, how the woman achieves permanently breaking the couple's love for each other as he continues to dream, the dancers on the stage act out the drama of the lover's break up. His dream fades into images of the instruments that will play his new composition. He dreams about the wild forest animals listening to his new composition and they start to play instruments on the stage with the dancers. Finally, his dream fades into the members of the whole Dreamville orchestra playing his music under the stars. He has dreamed a whole new story he'll be able to share with the people of Dreamville when he wakes.

Simon wakes up the next day and stretches his limbs. He detaches the dream catcher from his head and places the computer chip from the dream catcher into his portable hand held computer and listens to his new composition. His mother walks by and pokes her head in his room and says, "New composition son? It sounds serious." Simon hops out of bed and says, "Yeah, I've never dreamed about something so weird before. Here look at the dancers on the stage." He hands his portable computer to his mother. She watches the act, smiles at Simon and says, "Actually, Simon this is quite good. I can't wait for the production. Why don't you show your father?" His mother hands him back his portable computer with his dream stored in his permanent files and says, "I'll do just that! Thanks mom. What did you create in your dream mom?" Simon's mom gives him her portable computer and he watches her dream of a new line of clothing for the new summer season and says, "Great clothes mom. No wonder you're a fashion designer." He gives her back her portable computer and she says, "Thanks son." Simon and his mother head downstairs to the kitchen where his dad's reading the virtual newspaper. Simon walks up to him and gives him his portable computer and says, "Dad I'd like your opinion about my new musical." Mr. Dreamlee picks up his son's hand held computer, listens and watches the production based on Simon's dream. He looks at his son and says, "It's quite good. It's quite serious. How does the third woman break them up though?" He hands the hand held computer to his son and Simon replies, "See that's the thing, I didn't dream about that. It's like that part will be the second act. I guess I'll have to wait and see what I dream about tonight." His father smiles at him and says, "Well it'll be a great production son. I hope Principal Toombs doesn't make a stink about this one like the last one." Simon rolls his eyes and says, "I know, I mean I made two million dollars with my last dream. What's the reason he's such a doom and gloom, mean man?" Simon's mother looks at her husband, they have a sad look on their faces and Mr. Dreamlee says, "He wasn't always this way son. We're the same age. No one really knows what happened. He just changed overnight." His parents look at each other again and give each other a kiss. Simon covers his eyes with his hands and says, "Okay, let me know when it's safe to look again." They finish kissing and Mr. Dreamlee says, "Hey, do you want to watch what I dreamed about?" Simon takes his hands off his eyes and grabs his father's hand held computer and says, "I sure do!" His father says, "I dreamed about a prototype for a newer, faster way to catch people's dreams by eliminating the computer chip and attach people's heads right to their hand held computers." Simon's eyes are big with curiosity and he says "Wow dad, that's great. I can't wait for you to develop it." He hands his father back his hand held computer. His mother says, "Alright son, grab a chocolate chip muffin for breakfast. Here's your lunch. A blueberry and peanut butter sandwich and freshly squeezed orange juice. We've got to get going or you'll be late for school and we all know that's not acceptable." Simon looks at the time on the hovering clock and says, "Yeah, the last kid that got dropped off at school late got his dreams confiscated for a month and it was Mayor Alldream's son. You would think he'd be able to save his son from Principal Toombs but he couldn't. Almont was so sad." Simon and his mother quickly get into the solar powered hover car, another one of Mr. Dreamlee's inventions in the continuously evolving technological world of Dreamville and they hover to Dreamtrue School.

The Dreamlee's pull up in front of the school and Simon gets out of the car and says, "Have a good day mom!" She replies, "You too son!" Simon shuts the door to the hover car and walks up the sidewalk to his school. Principal Toombs stands at the front doors watching the students. Principal Toombs says, "Back to school kids. It's back to school Simon." Simon turns as he picks him out from all the kids around him. Simon's not sure what to say but replies, "Back to school Principal Toombs." Principal Toombs grabs his shoulders, turns Simon towards him and says, "What was that Simon. Are you giving me lip already on the first day of school?" Simon just looks at his yellow teeth, yellow eyes and pointy nose, he says, "No sir, Principal Toombs sir. I just repeated what you said sir." Principal Toombs releases his grip on Simon and points him towards the front door of the school. Relieved but scared that he might change his mind, Simon runs inside to his classroom. Simon walks into the classroom for the musically inclined. In Dreamville, school is divided by what the kids dream rather than by age and grade level. In Simon's class, the oldest student is eighteen and the youngest is five years old. Simon walks to a desk at the center of the class and sits down. He places his hand held computer in the pod on his desk and sets it to play on the big screen when his teacher, Miss LossDream, will call on him. He puts his lunch bag in his desk and waits for her to start the class. The kid in front of him turns around and says, "Pssst... I saw what Principal Toombs did to you. Are you okay?" Simon looks at Almont and says, "Oh yeah, I had forgotten already." Almont looks at him and says, "Don't. That's how he started with me last year. He's out to get you this year Simon." Almont turns around to face the class as Miss LossDream claps her hands to get the musically inclined students undivided attention and says, "Okay today I think we'll start with Simon Dreamlee's dream. Alright, Simon, play your creation." Simon smiles at her, he likes her, she's kind, encouraging, and nice. He didn't understand why she wasn't married. He presses play and says, "Enjoy!" The classroom fills with the music and the images of Simons dream are on the screen for the class to see. His dream stops playing and he presses stop and save on his hand held computer. He waits for Miss LossDream to criticize or praise his newest creation. She walks to the front of the class, looks at Simon and says, "That was really good. It brought tears to my eyes Simon. Truly I believe this will touch people's hearts. But I have one question. How does this woman manage to break up true love?" The whole class turns to look at Simon while he responds and he says, "That's the dilemma. I didn't dream about how this third woman broke them up. I think it'll be a dream I'll have later as a second composition." Shockingly, Miss LossDream runs out of the classroom crying. Almont turns around and says, "What was that about?" Simon looks at the screen on his desk and says, "I'm not sure but she gave me five stars out of five!" The whole class gets up and looks at his screen. Simon smiles at everyone, takes his hand held computer out of the pod and puts it in his pocket. Smiling, he can tell some of his classmates are happy for him as they smile back at him. Almont turns around and says, "Well I guess this month's production's all yours Simon." The lunch bell rings and his classmates disperse.

Simon and Almont have to pass the principal's office to get to in the lunchroom. As they walk by, Principal Toombs walks out in front of them and says, "Simon and Almont, well isn't this a sight. What are you two up to? What kind of mischief?" Almont gulps and freezes up. Simon just looks at him and says, "Nothing. We're not up to anything sir." Principal Toombs steps out of their way and they hasten their steps to go in the lunchroom. Principal Toombs yells, "I'm watching you two." They get to the lunchroom, walk in and find a seat to eat. Their school mates are verifying their dreams on their hand held computers. Simon looks at Almont who's visibly shaken by the confrontation and says, "I think you may be right. He's after me but I've done nothing wrong. Why do you think he's after me?" Almont says, "I don't know. I still don't know why he was after, and apparently, is still after me." Simon takes a bite of his sandwich and looks around the lunchroom and says, "Maybe it's because our dreams get the best reviews in the entertainment industry. You know, he never congratulates anyone on their success and he always laughs at those who don't succeed." Almont replies, "Jealousy, you think he's just jealous of you and me and well everybody." Simon says, "Yes. What else could it be?" Almont says, "I don't know. Your guess is as good as mine." The class bell rings and they get back to class passing by the science dreamers, the artistic dreamers, the theatre dreamers, the creative dreamers, the math dreamers and the miscellaneous dreamers to avoid going past the principal's office.

Back in their seats in their classroom, Miss LossDream enters the class and takes her seat behind her podium. Almont turns around and says, "Good idea taking the long way to get back." Simon nods his head and Almont turns back to the front of the class. Miss LossDream stands, everyone hushes and she says, "Class I've been impressed by all of your dreams. I reviewed them over the lunch period. With that said I have to choose the one that will make money and that will be Simon's composition. It has everything, orchestra, dancers, a great story with a potential sequel and intriguing drama. There'll be no need to tweak the music he composed either. It's a masterpiece Simon and I have already informed the dancers, the orchestra and the other teachers who all concur. Simon this production, without a doubt in my mind, is all yours. When you're ready to begin, we'll all be ready to start." Miss LossDream sits back down at her podium as they all look at Simon and wait for his response. Simon looks at everyone, smiles and says, "We should start right away so I'm thinking tomorrow morning in the school theatre. Please bring your instruments and your angelic singing voices. Thanks everyone and thank you Miss LossDream." The class claps, hoots and hollers. Miss LossDream says, "Alright, class dismissed. Everyone go home and until tomorrow." Everyone picks up their personal hand held computers and exit the classroom. Almont gets up and says, "See you tomorrow Simon." He leaves the class. Simon checks his pocket to make sure he has his hand held computer and hears an unusual, misplaced sound, he hears crying. He looks at Miss LossDream and sees tears streaming down her face. Simon walks up to her and asks, "Miss LossDream is there anything wrong?" She looks up and sees Simon standing there waiting for her to respond and she says, "No, Simon. I just have a touch of the cold that's all. Go home." He doesn't believe her but Simon walks out of the classroom to head home. He walks out the front door and gets in the hover car with his father. His father says, "Son, I read in the immediate virtual news that your dream's going to be produced. That's great news! Congratulations!" Simon looks out the window and can't help but not get the image of Miss LossDream crying out of his mind and says, "Yeah dad. It's great alright!" He spots Principal Toombs and Miss LossDream fighting in front of the school and watches her run away crying even more. Simon turns to his father and asks, "Dad, why has Miss LossDream never gotten married?" His father pulls the car up in hover mode, starts hovering home and says, "Well son that's a long story that really isn't my place to tell and besides it's her choice. We live in a free society son." Simon accepts the answer while his father parks the hover car in front of their family home. He gets out of the car and says, "It's just that today…" His father looks at him and says, "It's just that what son?" Simon doesn't want to embarrass his teacher so he makes up a tiny little fib and says, "It's just that I know I'm too young for her but if I could I'd marry her." His father laughs and puts his arm around his son as they walk into their house. His father says, "That's my boy!"

Once inside the house, Simon silently observes his parents interact together. He imprints in his memory the happiness they bring each other and their constant, yet gross, display of affection for each other with their kisses. He wishes this could be the same for Miss LossDream and wonders what he can do to help. He has his supper of apple pie with whip cream and chocolate milk made with fresh cow milk from their cow, Wendy, in the backyard and goes to the attic to survey the stars. He pulls out his hand held computer and brings up the virtual internet site with the constellations. He looks out of the attic window to see the stars. As usual, the sky's clear. He looks at the North Star, the big dipper, the little dipper and the Milky Way. Suddenly his orange female cat, Frankie Noodles, startles him by jumping on his telescopes and spinning it around in the stand. Simon startled says, "Go get, go downstairs Frankie Noodles." Frankie Noodles, the cat, just starts to purr and rub up against Simon's legs. Simon looks into his telescope to adjust it and stumbles on Principal Toombs house. The moonlight shines on the black monstrosity, the charcoal grey gargoyles and the black windows. "Meow…" Simon's cat meows and distracts him a bit from his observation but he starts to look again. Simon sees a shadowy figure walking up the sidewalk to Principal Toombs front door, then turns around and runs away. Simon whispers, "That was odd. No one would dare go near Principal Toombs house during the daytime, let alone at night. I wonder who that was." He hears his mother say, "Simon time for bed." Simon yells down, "Yes Mom." He goes to his bedroom and prepares for bed. He climbs in and both his parents poke their heads in his room and say, "Sweet dreams son!" Simon says, "Sweet dreams mom and dad!" As usual his dog, Boomboom Booya, jumps on his bed and sleeps at his feet. He attaches the dream catcher to his head and as per Dreamvillian tradition, once his head touches his pillow he falls to sleep.

While he sleeps, Simon's dream fades into a shiny, sparkly, silvery background as the dancers act out his story on stage with their ballerina movements. They move across the stage like angels dressed in white. The ballerinas exaggerate each movement with graceful elegance. They express their love for each other with their facial expressions. At the point, where the two lovers dance their way into a position that makes them look like their kissing on stage a bright light radiates from their souls and living, golden gargoyles fly around them. Unfortunately, the mysterious third woman enters the picture dressed in black and weaves a sheer black material around the male dancer to symbolize her expression of her poisonous love for him while the female dancer dressed in white starts to cry while she dances away in pain from her former lover. He begins frantic movements to escape the black material holding his heart and head while he's expressing his agony on his face. The mysterious evil woman unravels him and the male dancer's now dressed in black, his light dims and eventually goes completely out, his face's angry as he holds his head on the stage. The female dancer dressed in white enters onto the stage, she approaches her former lover and he turns his back on her. She dances her way with painful movements with facial expressions displaying her heart breaking, just as she's about to exit the stage, she pulls a red porcelain heart from her chest and drops it on the stage to symbolize her broken heart. The male dancer prances around the stage in agonizing movements as he suddenly stops and angrily looks at the audience, he pulls ashes from his chest and scatters them on the stage to symbolize he has no heart. The light dims on the stage and suddenly, the third woman who was on the stage observing her plan to break up the lovers being well executed, approaches the man and he pushes her to the ground, holds his head and runs off the stage with strong graceful ballet steps. She's alone in the center of the stage as the lights turn deep red, she looks out into the audience and rolls her body around and she laughs as the lights go out and no one can see the stage anymore. This symbolizes her joy that no one will be his lover if she's not the one he loves. The music Simon composed in his first dream ends a few seconds after the lights go out with a dramatic bang, silence and darkness fills the rest of his dream.

Chapter Two – Principal Toombs Confiscates Simon's Dreams

Thursday Morning, according to Dreamville's calendar, it's the first day of the fourth summer season. Simon wakes up to the sound of his cat, Frankie Noodles, purring as she walks across his chest, the birds singing and his dog, Boomboom Booya, barking at the cow, Wendy, in the backyard. He lifts Frankie Noodles off of him and sets her down on the floor. He detaches the dream catcher from his head, takes the computer chip from the dream catcher and inserts it in his hand held computer. He presses download, instantaneously his dream plays on the screen and he gets out of bed. His father pokes his head in his room and asks, "Good dream son?" Simon looks up at his father and replies, "Great, I know what to produce for the theatre now!" Mr. Dreamlee says, "That's great son. Let's watch the dreamed up production of yours on the virtual screen in the virtual room. Meet you there." He hears his father's footsteps go down the stairs. Simon looks out his bathroom window and breathes in the fresh air. He goes downstairs to the virtual screen room and his father and mother are waiting there with a bucket of popcorn. His mother says, "Go ahead son, put your dream in the virtual dream player." Simon places his hand held computer in the pod and says, "Play Simon's dream please." A tiny yawning figure of a girl visualizes before their eyes on the screen and says, "Oh, is this another one of Simon's great dreams. Alright, I, the virtual dream player, will play your dream. "She sits in the corner of the screen as the production plays for his parents. Stumped, Simon watches intensely to try and figure out how the woman breaks up true love but this dream doesn't answer this question. The virtual dream player stands up and announces, "Simon's dream is finished playing. Anyone else want to view their dream?" Simon looks at his parents and his mother says, "No not today Viadream. Thank you." The virtual dream player replies, "Alright, I have to say great dream Simon. Good bye until next time." The tiny virtual image fades away as she yawns again. Simon takes out his hand held computer from the pod, puts it in his pocket and asks his parents, "So what do you think?" His parents look at each other and his mother says, "I love it, the drama, the suspense, the music you composed is enthralling." His father says, "It's mature. I can't wait for the sequel to find out how the woman broke up true love." Simon smiles and then says, "That's the problem. What if I don't dream up the sequel with the answer? People are going to be disappointed." Simon's father says, "No they won't because the dream will come to you son. Now let's get to school and work." Simon walks to the front door and says, "I think I'll take my solar powered hover bike today. Bye." Simon's mom says. "Bye dear." Simon hovers along the bike hover pathway to school. Along the way every one of the adults wave, smile and congratulate Simon on his latest dream. Mrs. Dreammore and Mrs. LandDream say, "Congratulations Simon. I can't wait to see your dream in theatres." Simon replies, "Thank you, thank you." Mr. BottomDream says, "Good job chap." Simon replies, "Thanks Mr. BottomDream. See you at the theatre."

Once at school, he lowers his hover bike into the solar panel power grid in the hover bike parkade and gets off. Almont runs up to him and says, "Simon, I was beginning to think you weren't coming to school today. We better hurry to get inside before Principal Toombs targets us again." Simon replies, "The big bully." They walk up the sidewalk to the side door to avoid him while he stands at the front door. Once in the corridors of the school they take the long way around and see some amazing stuff being produced by the science dreamers. Simon says, "Wow look at that. What is that?" An older boy of fourteen named Rino DreamScifi answers him, "Simon Dreamlee. I hear we will be greatly entertained by your latest dream. Good for you. But we all know the sciences are the future and what you're looking at is a dream stopper that can filter out dreams just long enough to allow us to finish one project before dreaming up the next one." Almont smiles and says, "That's great. That's futuristic and convenient." Simon replies, "Yeah, it really is. I can't count how many times I've heard my mother say that she has to many dreams going on at the same time that she sometimes isn't sure her clothes will be ready by the time her runway shows start." Rino replies, "Why thank you Simon. I do value your opinion, especially since your father's the head science dreamer in Dreamville. And, I take back my comment; there'll always be place for entertainment." The bell rings and they all look at each other and start running to their classes.

Getting to their classroom late, Miss LossDream watches Simon and Almont sneak into the classroom while another student's dream plays on the big screen. They take their seats and their fellow classmates dream ends. The lights come on automatically and Miss LossDream stands in front of the class and says, "Jilla MusiDream that was an interesting piece of music that will certainly earn you recognition but unfortunately not from Simon and Almont. So I say Bravo to you Jilla. However, on a sour note, Simon and Almont, according to the school rules, I have to send you both to the principal's office." Principal Toombs sticks his head in the classroom and says, "Aha, I knew you two were up to no good this school term. Come with me." He enters the classroom, pinches their ears and walks them out of the classroom. Miss LossDream follows them out of the classroom and says, "Principal Toombs is that really necessary?" He turns to her with his yellow eyes, pointy nose, malicious grin and replies, "Yes Miss LossDream it is. It would do you some good to mind your business and get your head out of the overly blue sky once in a while." Miss LossDream says, "There was a time where you were happy. Do you remember that time?" She storms back into the classroom and Principal Toombs delights in the gloomy chaos he creates with a terrible laugh. "Ha-ha. Aha." He looks at the two boys with the same malicious grin and drags them by their ears to his office. All the way to the office, Simon and Almont both quietly express their pain, "Owe… Owe… Owe…Owe."

Once in his office, he sits them down in two ratty old wood chairs and says, "Your dreams. Hand them over." Simon asks, "All of them?" Principal Toombs leans forward right into Simon's face and says, "All of them. Your dreams are confiscated until I say you can have them back. Now look at the big star dreamer. Now hand them over." Simon can smell his breath. It smells like rotting apples. Principal Toombs looks at Almont as he gives him his hand held computer. Simon manages to sneak his computer chip out and into his pocket before he hands his hand held computer to Principal Toombs. Principal Toombs looks at Simon and says, "No funny stuff now. You're both going to sit here for the day and not a word out of either of you." Simon gulps as he watches Principal Toombs walk to his desk, put his dreams into a drawer and lock the drawer. He looks at them again. "Now I have a meeting today so don't try and get your dreams back or you'll set off the alarm. You see only my finger print opens this lock. Ha-ha… Ha-ha… Aha." He gets up and exits his office. Simon notices the secretary sitting in her ripped putrid green leather seat watching them out of the corner of her eye. He has never seen her before. She isn't like the rest of the town's people either. She's dressed in black, doesn't smile, she doesn't say anything while she sorts the science dreamers' computer chips. She sorts them into two piles, the ones that haven't been graded from the ones that have been graded. Shivering, Almont and Simon sit in their rickety chairs while the cold air of the office chills both of them. Simon looks around the room in the office and finds it odd there's not a single picture of Principal Toombs relatives, friends or even family pets. Instead, the two rooms are dark and gloomy with no sunlight with the only window painted black. Statues of miniature Gargoyles are everywhere in the room. These mini gargoyles look down on them with their fierce teeth, eyes and overall faces. There's a squeaking sound in the far left corner where Simon sees a poor mouse caged and running on a wheel. The secretary gets up to answer a floating phone message. The message says, "This is Principal Toombs Miss DreamNot. I'm calling to tell you that those two trouble makers stay in my office until the end of the day. I'll keep their dreams locked in my desk over night. Bye." Miss DreamNot looks at them and says, "Well you heard him. No sweet dreams for you tonight. Ha-ha... ha..." Simon couldn't help but notice the similarities between the two of them. Despite his observations, Simon's happy that he has his computer chip and smiles innocently at Miss DreamNot. She glares at him meanly, menacingly and says, "What do you have to smile about trouble maker? Don't answer. You're not allowed to talk." They sit in the office until the last bell of the day. Miss LossDream walks in the office and holds out her hands. Miss DreamNot says, "What do you think you're doing Miss LossDream?" She turns to her and replies with a smile, "Taking their hands and escorting them to their hover bikes so they can safely go home." Simon and Almont smile at each other, they get up and take her hands. They walk out of the office, out of the school to the hover bike parkade. Simon looks at Miss LossDream and says, "Miss LossDream, thank you but Principal Toombs confiscated our hand held computers with our dreams. He never said when will be getting them back. Do you think you could ask him?" Miss LossDream smiles at them both and says, "No one can ever truly take your dreams away from you." She looks around, looks back at them and says, "Here use these spare hand held computers until Principal Toombs gives you back yours." Almont relieved says, "Oh thank you Miss LossDream." Simon slips his computer chip out of his shirt and says, "Here Miss LossDream. I snuck my computer chip out before giving it to him. Take it and watch it. It's my dream of the complete production but I haven't dreamt about the sequel yet." She takes Simon's computer chip and puts it in her pocket. She says, "Tomorrow Simon, you're the boss. We started a little planning today but the big organizing is all yours. I'll watch this and gather the props. Good night boys. Sweet Dreams." She walks towards the school and enters the front doors. Almont looks at Simon and says, "I wish I had thought of taking my computer chip." Simon says, "You couldn't, he was looking right at you." Almont says, "Let's go home Simon." They get on their hover bikes and hover to their home. During their hover home, Simon asks, "Almont, have you ever seen Miss DreamNot before today?" Almont replies, "Only the time I was punished last year. But now that you mention it, I've never seen her around town though." Simon's intrigued by his answer and asks, "Does anyone know where she lives?" Almont's perplexed and answers, "No, no one knows where she lives and because she's more miserable than Principal Toombs no one has bothered to find out." Simon's more curious, "I think we should find out one day. Tomorrow's the summer festival. Let's follow her to her house after school." Almont looks at Simon and says, "Alright, I'm in." They reach the crossroads of Dreamway Street and ValleysDream Drive where they go in opposite directions. Almont yells, "See you tomorrow Simon." Simon replies, "Yeah, see you tomorrow Almont." Almont turns to his left and hovers towards his house. Simon stops at the end of his driveway, hovers and looks up the hill at Principal Toombs house. He turns left into his driveway and parks his hover bike in the back yard in the solar stand. He pets his dog, Boomboom Booya, the cow, Wendy, and looks again at Principal Toombs House. Simon quietly says, "I wonder how he and his secretary can be so unhappy when they live in the happiest place on earth." He walks into the kitchen of his home.

In the kitchen, Simon sees the hovering message board with a digital message from his mother. Simon says, "Speak." His mother's voice says, "Simon, dear your father and I are running late today. He's busy with his new invention and I have dream overload with my new clothing line so we'll see you when we get home. Oh yeah, there's a chocolate pie in the fridge for your supper. Love you." Simon walks to the fridge and takes out the pie. He starts to eat the chocolate pie piled with whip cream and chocolate shavings for his supper. While he eats he downloads the daily news to the virtual kitchen viewing screen. The news clown reporter says, "It's been another summery summer day in Dreamville and there's been a record number of dreams come true. Fashion Clothing Designer Mrs. Dreamlee's new summer line will be revealed tomorrow, being Friday, at the dreamers fashion show. Clothes will be worn by Dreamville's family of models the DreamModels. The event is titled; Wear the Dream. Mr. Dreamlee has revealed his new scientific invention that will enable us all to catch our dreams without the need of a computer chip and plug our heads directly into our hand held computers which will now be the size of computer chips. I guess teachers will have to find a new way to grade the kids. How dreamy is that? Mayor Alldream will be cutting the ribbon to open the dreamy summer festival tomorrow. Sweet Dreams!" He shuts the virtual news off and goes up to the attic for his daily star gazing. In a way Simon could be a scientist but that's not what he dreams about, therefore, this isn't his inclination.

In the attic, he looks out the window through his telescope. He hasn't changed the coordinates from the night before and he looks at Principal Toombs house. What he sees surprises him. He observes Miss DreamNot sneaking around Principal Toombs house. She's trying to look in his windows but she can't see through the thick black paint. She seems to be spreading some kind of powdery substance around his house and his yard but Simon can't make it out. She turns around and Simon can clearly see her face. She looks up and to Simon it looks like she's looking right back at him through his telescope. Startled, Simon backs away from his device. He shakes his head and says, "Nah, there's no way she can see me." He looks through his telescope but he can't find her anywhere in his yard. She's gone, like she disappeared into thin air. The streets of Dreamville are so well lit that there's no way she could have walked in the streets without his being able to see her. He moves his telescope everywhere to try and find her but he doesn't see her at all. Simon steps back from his telescope, and quietly says, "That was beyond weird." He decides to observe the stars again by looking up the planets. He powers up his telescope to view deeper into the galaxy. This time he looks for the planet of Mars. He spots the big red planet of Mars and compares it to the internet site on the hand held computer Miss LossDream gave him to use temporarily. His star gazing is going well until he hears a giant bang and faint voices that are screaming at the top of their lungs. The sounds are coming from Principal Toombs house. He quickly focuses his telescope towards the gloomy, scary house and yard. Looking through his telescope he sees Miss LossDream coming out of the house after slamming the door behind her and Mr. Toombs yelling, "Miss LossDream stop bothering me with what happened ten years ago. Now get out of my sight. Better yet get out of my yard." Miss LossDream yells back, "Please, you have to try and remember." Principal Toombs glares at her with his scary yellow eyes and screams, "I refuse to remember. Now just leave before… Before I…" He sighs and walks back into his house. Miss LossDream just watches him walk into his house and slowly walks down to her hover car and sobs in her car. Finally, she drives away towards her house. Simon lifts his head from his telescope and is more confused than ever. He says to himself, "What did Miss LossDream mean by telling him to try and remember?" Simon sits in the attic petting Frankie Noodles with the scene that just took place re-running in his mind. Suddenly, he hears his mother and father pull up the hover way driveway with the hover car and park. He gets up and runs downstairs to meet them at the front door.

They walk in the front door smiling and laughing. Mrs. Dreamlee says, "Why Charles Dreamlee I had no idea you were unveiling your invention today. I'm so proud of you!" Mr. Dreamlee blushes and says, "What about you Mirabélla and your new fashion line. I thought you were waiting until this summer was over and unveiling your new line when the new summer begins. I'm proud of you too honey!" They give each other a little kiss. Simon covers his eyes with his hands and says, "Tell me when it's safe to look again." His parents look at him and laugh. Simon's mom says, "And we're the proudest of you Simon! How was school today?" Simon uncovers his eyes, follows them into the kitchen and tells them what happened, "I… Almont and I got our dreams confiscated by Principal Toombs because of a new rule that we cannot be late for class. We didn't do it on purpose. We were distracted by one of the science dreamers dream come true. He dreamt and fabricated a machine that can stop dreams until us dreamers are ready for our next big dream." Mr. Dreamlee looks at his son and says, "Well that's just great. A machine to stop dreams until you need or want to dream them. That's ingenious!" Mrs. Dreamlee smiles and says, "That's completely something I need. I dream up so many clothes that I sometimes can't keep track of which ones have come true and which ones haven't." Simon's father says, "So amazing what we can dream isn't it son." Simon looks at them, rolls his eyes and says, "Yes, yes his invention will be the future and all of that will entail his dream come true but mom, dad, please focus. What about my dreams? Principal Toombs has my hand held computer." Mr. Dreamlee replies, "Forget about it. I patented and marketed my new dream catcher today and I brought home one for your lovely mother." Mrs. Dreamlee says, "Thank you dear." Mr. Dreamlee says, "Your welcome my love. I also brought you one too my son. So out with the old technology and bring in the new!" Simon says, "So my sneaking my computer chip out of my hand held computer wasn't necessary?" Mr.

Dreamlee replies, "Not really. With my new dream catcher invention, I've eliminated the computer chip and they'll come with a computer chip sized hand held computer that will still function with your pod stations at your school and even here at home. But that's not even the best part. The best part is that it's voice commanded and virtual so when you want to research the stars for example you tell it to search and the virtual image will appear before your eyes. Plus your dreams will be virtual images as well as stored for life in the computer. Ha! Great!" Simon asks, "But won't anyone have access to my dreams with voice command?" Simon's dad looks at him and answers, "You would think so but no. I invented a voice sensory mechanism that imprints only the dreamer's voice from the very first moment the dreamer has their first dream. Great! Yes?" Simon's mom says, "Perfect, a really great invention. Isn't it Simon?" Simon thinks about it for a moment and says, "Yes, a great invention. I guess I'll find out tomorrow how the teachers plan to grade us now." Mr. Dreamlee smiles and says, "Ah well that won't change all that much. They won't be collecting your computer chips to grade you. Instead, Miss LossDream will grade you on the spot, a much quicker, simpler and efficient way to grade students." Simon looks at his dad, "Thanks dad for my new dream catcher. It's great!" Simon's mom says, "Well son it's time for bed unless there's anything you wanted to talk about." She smiles at him and his father smiles at him too. Simon decides not to tell them what he observed through his telescope. Besides he doesn't really understand what he saw. Simon replies, "No, there's nothing else I want to talk about so I'm going to bed." He walks upstairs to his room and takes his old dream catcher and puts in the technological recycling chute and watches as it gets sucked down the chute. He opens his new dream catcher and attaches it to his head. He looks at the foot of his bed where his dog, Boomboom Booya, is already sleeping and puts his head on his pillow. In less than a half a second, he's sound asleep. His parents stick their heads in his room and say, "Sweet dreams son!" They notice he's already sleeping and shut his bedroom door.

While Simon sleeps snuggly in his bed, he drifts into dreamland. The notes of his latest composition vividly and loudly fill his dream. The same three dancers dance and act out the story on the same stage which looks like stars and moonlight during a dreamy warm summer night. This time, live, colorful, beautifully scented plants adorn the stage. The plants are wild rose bushes, wild lilies, wild sunflowers, wild blue bells and an orchard of apple trees. The two lovers radiate with light while they dance expressing their love for each other. The music is light, bouncy, and full of love. At the moment where the evil third woman enters the stage and envelopes the male dancer in the black material, the plants begin to whither, shrivel and die as his light goes out. The music becomes low, dramatic and damning. In the final moment, the once living statues of gargoyles start to pop up everywhere on the stage but are now frozen. While the evil woman laughs, the stage goes black. The music briefly continues to end dramatically and loudly, signaling the end of the couple's true love and the beginning of the man's unhappiness. Suddenly in his dream there are voices speaking out of the darkness but there are no faces. The voices say, "Still no explanation how the evil woman accomplishes to execute her plan to end true love. Simons dream isn't happy. It doesn't suit the attitude of the town's people of Dreamville. No, I disagree, his dream, without question, is evolutionary." With these last criticisms and praise, Simon's dream goes black and soundless for the rest of the night but he still sleeps soundly.

Chapter Three – Principal Toombs Scheme

The next morning, Friday morning, Simon wakes to Boomboom Booya licking his face. Simon pushes his dog away and says to his dog, "Stop that boy." He gets up, stretches and detaches the dream catcher head set from his head and from the computer chip sized hand held computer. He says, "Play Simon's dream titled true love broken." The virtual image of his dream plays before his eyes with his music and everything. He's amazed by the accuracy and vividness of the virtual movements of the ballerinas as they dance around his room. His father's head is in the doorway and says, "Great, isn't it son!" Simon looks at his dad and replies. "It's evolutionary dad!" His dad rushes down the stairs but loudly says, "Thanks son. Sorry I won't be having breakfast with you. I have to get to work early today. Love you son bye." Simon hears his dad get in the solar powered hover car and hover off to his office. Simon puts his new tiny computer in his pocket, pats his pocket with his hand and says to himself, "Handy." Simon smiles at himself in the mirror and says to his dog, "Okay boy, time to go downstairs. Come on Boomboom Booya." Simon and his dog go downstairs.

Once downstairs, he goes in the kitchen and he lets his dog out the back door. Simon's mom walks in dressed in her most fashionable creation and says, "I'll see you later at the summer festivities Simon but for now I have to run! Bye!" Simon turns around and says, "Bye mom!" He grabs himself a freshly made candied apple and eats it for breakfast. He gets his hover bike and makes his way to school. Almont comes up to the intersection and yells, "Hey wait up Simon." Simon slows down and waits for him to catch up and says, "Morning Almont. You'll never guess what I witnessed last night while looking through my telescope." Almont's visibly intrigued and says, "I probably can't guess so why don't you tell me." Simon looks around and sees no one's around and starts telling Almont what he thinks he saw. Simon talks about what he thinks he saw while they hover to school up to the point where they park their hover bikes in the hover craft parkade. They walk up the sidewalk to the front doors of the school. Almont exclaims, "Wow, really. You saw both Miss DreamNot and Miss LossDream at Principal Toombs house last night. That's weird." Simon replies, "Tell me about it. I was perplexed last night trying to figure out why Miss LossDream of all people was at his house. I'm still trying to figure out what she means by telling him to remember." Almont says, "Yeah, remember what? That's the question. Do you think any of the adults would know what they were fighting about?" Simon replies, "Good question but I don't think any of them would tell us even if they did know the reason." They walk to the front doors of Dreamtrue School and just about make it inside when Principal Toombs stops them and says, "Well, well, well the trouble making duo. There might be no reason for me to give you back your obsolete hand held computers but I'm still keeping both my eyes on you two. Now get to class on time today. Go." Once he was done talking they nodded their heads and quickly ran to class. They sit in their seats and catch their breath. The bell rings to indicate the start of class and Miss Loss Dream walks into the classroom. She stands in front of the class and says, "Today we start making Simon's dream come true but I believe we need a little more clarification from you Simon, a little more direction." Simon looks at her and says, "Ah yeah, I will play what I dreamt last night and this is what I want to make come alive." Simon puts his tiny computer chip sized hand held computer in the docking pod and just like his father said it starts playing on the big screen once he says, "Play my latest dream." The class watches in awe and thirty minutes later, Simons dream gets a standing ovation from his fellow musically inclined classmates. Miss LossDream stands in front of the class as the lights automatically come back on and says, "Open the curtains." The big screen hovers up to the ceiling and the virtual illusion wall that was behind it turns into a curtain and draws itself back revealing the enormous orchestra and theatre room. Miss LossDream says, "Let the dream come true." She directs everyone to the seating area in the theatre room.

Once in the theatre room everyone waits for Simon to speak and give them their direction. Simon walks onto the stage and sits on the edge. He gets up and sits at the grand piano and plays his composition. Everyone claps as he finishes his piece. He says, "I will be the pianist and accompanying me..." Miss LossDream says, "I couldn't agree more with you." Simon walks to the edge of the stage and sits again. Looking out at his fellow musically inclined dreamers, he says, "Almont playing the flute, Henrietta Dreamery playing the harp and Hughes Dreamy playing the acoustic guitar will accompany me while I play the piano. This combination of sounds will portray the light and airy love portion of my music piece. We'll play while the two dancers portray the true lovers on the spectacular stage." He looks at a classmate of his and says, "Michella Daydream will play the violin for the dramatic portion. She'll start to play when the evil woman enters the stage and her violin playing will get more intense while the evil woman's plan to corrupt the love between the lovers succeeds." Miss LossDream says, "Wonderful ideas Simon. Continue." He says, "I want a soft continuous drum beat that will get louder during key points of the performance. This sound will symbolize the beating hearts of the lovers but the soft constant drum beat will stop when the female dancer dressed in white shows her heart is broken. I think that Jonas DrumDreamer should play the drums." Miss LossDream says, "Oh bravo Simon. This will be the best dream come true you've dreamt up yet." Simon says, "Thank you. I need the background to be silvery, shiny and lit like the night sky and a spot light for the pale moonlight and two bright spotlights for the light that radiates from the lovers bodies and souls." He stops talking when he sees the dreamers of dance walk in the theatre. Miss LossDream says, "These are the dancers from the dance inclined class. The background will be built by the miscellaneous dreamers. They already viewed your dream and their all on board." Simon smiles and says, "Really, that's great. Well lets all go out there and break a leg everybody as the expression goes in theatre!" Miss LossDream says, "Oh that's true. They've been saying that for centuries. Simon's right everyone let's make this dream come true!" Everyone claps and start their roles. The musicians practice the dancers imitate the choreography from Simon's dream, and the miscellaneous dreamers build the set. Miss LossDream oversees the whole process with joy. The day goes by extremely well, so well, no one notices Principal Toombs poking his head in the theatre to mock them while they practice.

Grumpy Principal Toombs walks back into his gloomy office and says to Miss DreamNot, "Those musically inclined trouble makers will not be making Simon's dream come true. I'll make sure of it." Miss DreamNot asks, "How do you plan to stop them?" Principal Toombs looks at his blackened window as if he was looking outside and says, "By turning the town against his production." The lunch bell rings and the kids start walking by his office to get to the lunchroom. Principal Toombs storms out of his office past Simon and Almont. He glares at them and says, "Enjoy your dream coming true while you still can." He continues down the hall and around the left corner. Simon and Almont watch him as he goes down the hall with his very sinister, hunched over walk. He walks into the theatre room. Almont says, "What do you think he meant by that comment?" Simon replies, "I don't know but I'm sure it's something evil." They walk towards the doorway to the theatre room and listen at the door. Simon whispers, "Let's listen. We're bound to find out what he meant by that strange comment." They wait silently to hear the conversation between Principal Toombs and Miss LossDream. They see them talking but they cannot hear them. Almont says, "Miss LossDream looks upset." Simon says, "She sure does. I wonder what he's telling her." Principal Toombs turns towards the doorway and starts walking out of the theatre room. Fearing being caught eaves dropping; Simon and Almont quickly run to the lunchroom.

In the lunchroom, they sit and take out their lunches. Almont says, "Principal Toombs is up to something." Simon replies, "I agree and I think that somehow Miss LossDream and Miss DreamNot are entangled in his web of scheming. We have to find out what he's scheming and we still have to follow Miss DreamNot home to find out where she lives." Almont replies, "I'm in, anything to figure out why in Dreamville those two are so miserable." Simon says, "Yeah there has to be a reason and a way to help them or, if we have to, expose them and their evil plan." Almont asks, "Do you think he's planning to destroy Dreamville?" Simon replies, "There's no way to be sure yet, but my parents said he's been principal here for the past ten years and he's been this way the whole time. Ten years is more than enough time to plan an attack on the citizens of Deamville. Technically, I think he already has tried by always trying to destroy our dreams from coming true but he's never succeeded yet." Almont says, "The day he starts stopping our dreams will be a scary day indeed."

In the meantime, in the theatre room, Principal Toombs turns back to Miss LossDream and says, "That's my final decision. You'll not sway me, let alone the overly cheery people of this sickening town. I assure you I'm right this time. Simon's dream will not come true." Miss LossDream says, "Just because you are bitter, mean and decrepit and your dreams render you talentless doesn't give you the right to constantly try and destroy the dreams of the children of Dreamville, especially, the talented ones, although, they are all talented." Principal Toombs laughs evilly and replies, "The founders of Dreamville would beg to differ with you Miss

LossDream, and you see all dreams come true must absolutely, without question and undeniably be cheery and positive. Simon's latest dream, even you can't deny, is dramatic, dark and ends negatively. Therefore, Miss LossDream with this doctrine as my tool to destroy Simon's dream come true, I will succeed in darkening and dashing one child's dreams. Ha… Ha-ha." Miss LossDream replies, "But he will most certainly dream about the sequel which will undoubtedly end happy, full of love and positive just like members of parliament would want." Principal Toombs yellow eyes grow wide and he says, "Why that's a great idea I thought of. I'll present his dream to the esteemed members of parliament who will surely ban it from ever coming true. Ha, ha, ha. Thank you Miss LossDream, that will be all for today." He turns and walks out of the classroom. Miss LossDream sits down in her chair and sobs until the bell rings. Principal Toombs walks into his office and says, "Miss DreamNot I have the perfect solution to my dilemma. Get the first representative of parliament on the line. I will present Simon's dream to them and ha, ha, ha, they will ban his dream from coming true." Miss DreamNot says, "If you succeed, this will be an apocalyptic event in the history of Dreamville. Ha, ha. Ha. Do you think your plan will work?" Principal Toombs replies, "Ha, ha, ha… Absolutely, leave it to me Miss DreamNot." They turn and watch the students walk by the office laughing and talking happily. Principal Toombs says, "They'll soon fear sharing their dreams with anyone."

The bell rings and the students proceed to their classes. Taking the long way around, Simon and Almont get to class last but on time. They take their seats and prepare to watch one of their classmates dreams on the big screen. Miss LossDream says, "Now class we'll listen and view Hughes dream. Everyone enjoy the upbeat, modern, mainstream genre of music he's inclined to dream about and create. Go ahead Hughes." Hughes replies, "Yes Miss LossDream." Hughes presses play and they view a group of electric guitar playing teenagers perform their upbeat, happy song titled; Dance Like a Dreamvillian. While teenaged spectators dance and scream as they chant the catchy lyrics. The lyrics are clever, easy to remember, enticing and like the notes on the music sheet paper, the words to Hughes lyrics float on the screen in front of the musically inclined class. Simon bobs his head to the funky beat of the music while Almont hums along with the tune. The girls chant the refrain and the boys play air guitar until the small concert is over.

Dance, Dance, Dance,
Dreamville,
Dance like a
Dreamvillian,
Oh Hey, Oh Hey!
A Dreamer's inclination's to
Oh Hey, Oh Hey!

Turn, Turn, Turn,
Dreamville,
Turn like a
Dreamvillian,
Oh Hey, Oh Hey!
A Dreamer's inclination's to
Oh Hey, Oh Hey!

Jump, Jump, Jump,
Dreamville,
Jump like a
Dreamvillian,
Oh Hey, Oh Hey!
A Dreamer's inclination's to
Oh Hey, Oh Hey!
Oh Hey, Oh Hey!

A Dreamer's inclination's to
Oh Hey, Oh Hey!
Oh Hey, Oh Hey!
Oh Hey, dance, Oh Hey,
Like a Dreamvillian.
Oh Hey!

Hughes dream ends and the class claps, cheers, whistles and chant the lyrics. Miss LossDream gets up in front of the class and says, "Well that's it for today class. I'll see you all tomorrow. Sweet Dreams!" Almont turns to Simon and says, "Well are we still going through with the plan." Simon says, "Yes, we have no other choice." Almont gulps and replies, "Alright then, I'll follow your lead." Simon and Almont get out of their seats and walk towards the door. Miss LossDream stands up from her seat and says, "Oh Simon, I need to speak with you for a moment." Simon looks at Almont and turns around to face Miss LossDream. Almont waits just outside the door in the hallway. Miss LossDream walks up to Simon, puts her hand on his shoulder and says, "I'm afraid there's been a major issue raised about your dream coming true. Simon according to Dreamville's centuries old law, your dream may not be happy enough to be producible. I'm afraid that Principal Toombs has found a loophole in your case to actually succeed at destroying your dream. I'm sorry. I can't see anything that we can do about his decision." Simon replies, "But how can that be. This is Dreamville. We thrive on our dreams coming true. And the voices in my dream, everyone heard them. They said my dream, and you agreed, is evolutionary and progressive." Miss LossDream smiles and says, "You're right Simon. Perhaps what we should do is arrange to present your dream before parliament for their review and let them overturn Principal Toombs decision." Simon asks, "That's great. How soon can this parliament meeting take place?" Miss LossDream says, "Well it turns out that Principal Toombs is already arranging a hearing for Monday morning and won't he be surprised to see you, me and all the musically inclined dreamers there to plead your case." Simon nods his head and says, "Thank you Miss Loss Dream. I'll see you there Monday morning! Sweet dreams." Simon runs out of the class and bumps into Almont who's waiting in the corridor.

In the hallway, they shake off the initial shock of bumping into each other and run to just outside of the principal's office. Simon whispers, "Good they're not gone yet. Let's go outside and wait by our hover bikes. Come on." Almont nods his head and they walk out the front door of the school to their hover bikes. Almont says, "We better find something out because I'm missing my dad cut the dreamy red ribbon at the summer festivities." Simon says, "Yeah well, I'm missing my mother's launch of her new dreamy fashion clothing line." They watch as Principal Toombs walks out the front door and glares at them. He walks to his hover car which he has also painted black except for the windows and hovers in the direction of his house. Almont says, "We missed her leaving." Simon says, "No we didn't miss her leaving, look over there." Simon points at the side door. Miss DreamNot's exiting the school from the side door. Simon gets on his hover bike and says, "Okay here we go Almont." Almont gets on his hover bike and they wait to see which direction she goes. She gets in her very dirty, un-kept and dated hover car and hovers towards the woods. Simon and Almont look at each other and signal to each other to start following. They follow her down the forbidden road and the only known road out of Dreamville into the surrounding forest.

Almont says, "I don't know about this Simon. This is the forbidden part of the forest where the wild animals have been documented as attacking Dreamvillians." Simon says, "That's why it's interesting that she doesn't live in Dreamville. Look where she's going." Miss DreamNot pulls into a yard with a small shack made of grey wood and fogged up windows. She parks her hover car, gets out and carries a large box inside her shack. Simon says, "We have to get closer. We have to find out what's in that box." Almont nods his head in agreement, takes a big gulp and says, "We better leave out hover bikes here so she doesn't hear us approaching." Simon says, "Good idea." They park their hover bikes and tiptoe as quietly as possible to her house. Once at her house they tiptoe around to a side window and peek inside.

Inside Miss DreamNot's house, they see one small room with one little room for a bathroom, a single rocking chair fashioned out of broken branches and a stump for a table. There's a fire pit and a decent bed in the far corner of the room. Standing at the window, Simon spots Miss DreamNot and the mysterious box. Simon whispers, "She's over there." Almont whispers, "I see." Standing by her stump, she sits in her rocking chair and starts to hum a tune. Simon whispers, "Uh, she must be tone def." Almont nods his head in agreement. Miss DreamNot suddenly says, "All these obsolete computer chips of dreams will not be wasted. Not if they can help me, Miss DreamNot, have my revenge. Ah, justice at last will be mine after ten years." Standing out of the window, Almont steps on a very dry twig and it loudly cracks making the black crows in the trees fly away. Miss DreamNot says, "What was that? Is there someone out there? You dare to spy on me." Simon says, "Quick let's get back to our hover bikes before she spots us." They run back to their bikes and hover away just as Miss DreamNot runs out her door yelling, "I see you there, You stupid, eaves dropping, conniving little trouble makers. I'll find out who you are and you'll be sorry." She shakes her fist at them as they hover away. Hovering back the way they came as fast as they can, Almont hovers into an air pocket and flips off of his bike. Almont screams, "Whoa, ah. Wait up Simon." Simon turns around on his hover bike and sees Almont on the ground while his hover bike spins around and around in the air pocket. Simon asks, "Are you alright Almont?" Almont signals him to come over and says, "Yeah I'll be fine. Luckily this soft moss broke my fall. Can you get my hover bike out of that air pocket?" Simon says, "Sure thing." Simon pushes a button on his hover bike. A pair of robotic hands comes out of the front of his hover bike. The robotic hands grab a hold of the spinning bike and pull the bike out of the air pocket. The robotic hands pick Almont up off of the ground and sit him on his bike.

Simon smiles and Almont says, "Thanks Simon. We better get back though. It's dark and the wild, untamable wolves will soon come out of the woods." Suddenly they hear, "Ahooo, Ahooo!" They see a pack of wolves running out of the woods in their direction. They look at each other and start hovering at full throttle while the hungry wolves chase them back up the forbidden road to Dreamville. The sides of the road are filling with the shiny eyes of the forest creatures as they zoom by them. The wolves cease their pursuit once they reach the very edge of the forest wall. "Ahooo…Ahooo…" As their hearts beat fast, Simon and Almont don't stop their hastened pace until they reach the intersection that separates them as they head to their homes.

Once at the intersection, they stop and hover for a few moments. Almont says, "That was close. I never want to do that again. To think we almost became those wolves supper." Always remaining focused, Simon says, "She's definitely up to something and we already know Principal Toombs bringing my dream in front of parliament on Monday so we need to try and find the missing puzzle pieces. We need to find out what happened here in Dreamville ten years ago." Almont replies, "I'm with you but not tonight. I have to get home before my dad does or else I could be in trouble for disobeying him. Sweet dreams Simon." Almont starts to hover away and Simon yells back, "Sweet dreams Almont." Simon slowly hovers towards his house staring at the hill with Principal Toombs big black house. He tries to figure out the connection between him and Miss DreamNot. He no longer thinks Miss LossDream's involved but still wonders what she was doing there that night. He stops and hovers at the end of his house's hover way driveway and hears his mother, "Simon, dear. Where have you been?" Simon hovers up the hover way and replies, "Oh I've been hovering around doing nothing in particular." He parks his hover bike in the solar stand and walks in the house with his mother following right behind him. Mr. Dreamlee says, "Son, you're finally home. We need to talk to you."

Sitting around the stainless steel kitchen table, Simon's parents silently look at Simon. Simon smiles at them, waiting to be punished when his mother finally says, "We received a virtual call from Principal Toombs. He's communicated his dislike of your dream quite clearly and is attempting to boycott it from becoming true. Now we let him know that we disagree with him." Simon tries to say, "I know but…" Mr. Dreamlee interrupts and says, "However, Miss LossDream spoke to us both at the summer festivities and we agree with her and we'll both take time off of our dreams coming true, work, and we'll be by your side at the parliamentary hearing. We support you son so keep dreaming."

Simon smiles at them and replies, "That's great mom, dad. That's really all I could ask you to do for me. I have a question I want to ask you. I've asked it before but you didn't answer me." Mrs. Dreamlee looks at her husband and says, "What's your question dear?" Simon takes a few seconds to form his words in his head before asking and finally asks, "What happened here in Dreamville ten years ago?" Mr. Dreamlee replies, "Nothing. Nothing, you should be concerned about. Now it's your bedtime son. Go to bed. Sweet dreams!" While his parents smile at him Simon gets up from the table and starts going upstairs. Simon turns around and says, "Sweet dreams mom and dad!" His mother waves at him and says, "Sweet dreams son!" Simon climbs the stairs and goes into his bedroom. He looks out his window at the backyard and wonders about what happened ten years ago. He closes his window and sits on his bed. He climbs under the covers and pets his dog, his cat and imitates his bird, Allegretto's chirp. Simon says to his animals, "Well sweet dreams all." He attaches the dream catcher to his head and because his head is already resting on his pillow he's instantly sleeping and dreaming.

Simon sleeps soundly as the music of his to be debated composition and theatre piece are dancing off the music sheet. He dreams the same scene as his past two dreams but this time his music has lyrics. His lyrics tell a story with little explanation about how the third woman destroyed true love. The singers float above the dancers as their angelic voices sing their story titled; True Love, Broken.

A man, a woman, meet.
Stars glimmer.
Smiling,
Laughing,
Holding hands,
Their love's attractive.
Their love's true.

A man, a woman, meet.
Moonlight shines.
Dancing,
Spinning,
Gazing eyes,
Their love's powerful.
Their love's pure.

Their love's meaningful.
Their love's true.

A man, a woman, meet.
Wild flowers aroma,
Romancing,
Touching,
Kissing lips,

A man, a woman, meet.
Animals frolic.
Un-separating,
Embracing,
Loving souls,
Their love's powerful.
Their love's true.

A man, a woman, meet.
Pounding hearts,
Running,
Hugging,
Separating never,
Their love's powerful.
Their love's pure.
Their love's meaningful.
Their love's true.

The man, another woman,
Darkness surrounds.
Fighting,
Arguing,
Feels Disgusting,
Their love's powerful.
Their love's true.

The man, another woman,
Blackness,
Coldness,
Her jealousy,

Their love's powerful.
Their love's true.

The man, the woman, meet.
Plants whither,
Pushing,
Shoving,
Ceases to beat,
Their love's powerful.
Their love's true.

The man, the woman, meet.
Moonlight shines.
Cold,
Bitter,
True love, broken,
The woman backs away.
Light shines.
Heart shatters.
She's gone.
The man stands.
Light dies.
Heart, dust,
Loveless,

The other woman,
In the darkness,
Watches,
Laughs,
True Love, Broken,
Miserable,
Alone,
Dark days and nights,
Never end.

The final moments of Simon's dream fades to nothing, darkness, loneliness and the famous question still remains unanswered.

Chapter Four – Interrupted Summer Festival

Simon wakes up the next morning, Saturday Morning, quickly detaches the dream catcher from his head and says, "Gross they kiss. Gross... Gross and extremely gross kissing in my dream." Simon's mother sticks her head in the door and asks, "What was that dear?" Simon looks at her and replies, "Nothing mom. Nothing at all, everything's fine." She says, "Alright, well get ready to go to the summer festivities." Simon's father yells up the stairs from downstairs, "Come on you two. We'll be late." Simon and his parents get in their hover car and hover to the Dreamville festivities outdoor center. While hovering, Simon remarks, "Have you ever noticed that Principal Toombs and Miss DreamNot never attend the festivities?" Simon's father says, "Miss DreamNot? How do you know Miss DreamNot?" Simon looks at his father in the rear view mirror and replies, "She's Principal Toombs secretary at my school. Why?" Mrs. Dreamlee looks at her husband and they give each other a strange look. She says, "No reason dear. No reason at all. Oh look we're here! Let's all enjoy the summer festivities. Simon you're the pianist today and you're playing your last three dreams come true for the town. Oh but not the one being debated Monday. Alright, smiles!" Mr. Dreamlee parks the car and they all get out. Simon goes to the musically inclined dreamer's festivities outdoor section to set up for his piano pieces. Simon whispers, "Okay well I'll concentrate on having fun this weekend."

In the musically inclined outdoor section he spots Almont. While cleaning his flute, Almont smiles at Simon as he approaches. Simon smiles back and says, "I'm the pianist today." Almont says, "I'm playing the flute with Jilla. She's playing the harp. We're playing her dream come true titled, Dreamy Butterflies." Simon says, "Really, that's great. Aren't you going to play any of your compositions today?" Almont says, "Tomorrow. I'll be playing them tomorrow." Simon looks around and says, "I dreamt about lyrics to my piece last night. The lyrics still don't answer the question of who is the mysterious evil woman and how she destroys true love." Almont says, "Really? Wow, that will be the most complete dream come true ever Simon. Oh yeah, too bad that question isn't answered." Simon says, "That's not the worst part though. The worst part, they kiss." Almont's facial expression clearly indicates his disgusts. Almont says, "Gross, gross, that's sick. Which ones kiss?" Simon rolls his eyes and says, "The true lovers of course." Almont says, "Oh yeah, that makes sense." Simon sees Miss LossDream signaling everyone to the stage. Everyone takes their places to begin the outdoor summer festivities. Miss LossDream says, "Alright, all you dreamy musicians it's time to be entertainers for the summer festival. Simon will start us off." Simon starts to play his pieces. Miss LossDream announces, "First, his renowned Funky Pink Sky, followed by his famous Cloudless Dream and finally, his most famous piece, Hover Bike Mania."

Funk, funk, funk,
Funky Pink
In the sky,
Sky, sky, sky,
Oh my, that sky.

Look, look, look.
Pink funk
Up high.
In that funky
Pink sky,

Sky, sky, sky,
Oh my, that sky.
Everyone
Look at that funky
Pink Sky,

Funk, funk, funk,
Funky Pink
Sky,
Oh my, that sky.

It's a blue, blue
Ceiling
Cast over my dream.
Cloudless dream,
Cloudless dream,
Cloudless dream,

It's a bright, bright
Room,
In my dream,
Cloudless dream,
Cloudless dream,
Cloudless dream,

It's a sunny, sunny
Day
In my dream,
Cloudless dream,
Cloudless dream,
Cloudless dream,

It's a cheery, cheery
Fun
In my dream,
Cloudless dream,
Cloudless dream,
Cloudless dream,
I dream a cloudless dream.

I'm a hovering.
Just a hovering,
Hovering all over,
Hover bike,
Hover bike mania.

We're hovering.
Just a hovering,

Hovering all over,
Hover bike,
Hover bike mania.

Everywhere hovering,
Nowhere hovering,
Hovering dream,
Hover bike,

Hover bike mania.
Hover bike,
Hover bike,
Hover bike mania.

Miss LossDream says, "All three are short theatre pieces come true. Plus, all three are cheery, happy and playful beloved by the Dreamvillians." She claps along with the rest of the audience. Mrs. TwoDreams says, "I couldn't agree with you more Miss LossDream but, and perhaps you have the answer on every Dreamvillian's mind. Isn't it true that Simon Dreamlee's latest dream in the process of becoming true, well, is completely against the ancient doctrine of Dreamville?" Miss LossDream looks at Mrs. TwoDreams and replies, "That's up for debate on Monday. Tune in on the virtual parliamentary debates and decide for your selves." Miss LossDream walks away from Mrs. TwoDreams, sits down and waits for Almont and Jilla to play their musical piece. Simon gets off the stage and sits by Miss LossDream. Simon asks, "Miss LossDream, how long has Miss DreamNot been Principal Toombs secretary?" Miss Loss Dream turns to Simon and says, "Well that's an odd question to ask." She stands up in a hurry and quickly walks out of the tent. Simon whisper, "That was an odd reaction to a simple question. I have to talk to Almont. We need to find out more clues."

Dreamily flying,
Showing their colors,
Bright, wonderful colors,
Dreamy Butterflies,
I ask them why,
Do they fly away?
From me,

They say,
We're colorfully,
Fancy free,

Oh those dreamy butterflies.
Dreamy butterflies,
Dreamily flying by,
With wings of color,
Dreamy butterflies,
Dreamy butterflies,
Stay here with me.

Almont and Jilla finish their musical piece. Almont comes off the stage, Simon rushes to stop Almont before he decides to leave and says, "Almont I need to talk to you." Almont puts away his flute and says, "Okay. What is it?" Simon says, "Not here. Let's go somewhere." Almont nods his head and follows Simon out of the outdoor festival center. Standing under a tree at the edge of the outdoor festivities centre, Simon says, "I've asked my parents and Miss LossDream about Miss DreamNot and all of them reacted peculiarly. The adults are hiding something." Almont says, "Do you have any idea what?" Simon says, "No but I'm hoping that hearing I have to attend on Monday will provide me some answers. Hey look… Is that Principal Toombs?" Almont turns around, gulps and says, "Principal Toombs at the summer festivities. Something's terribly wrong." They watch him enter the musically inclined outdoor room. They run into the outdoor room. They see that he has taken over the stage and grabbed a hovering microphone from the super famous forty five year old Dreamilee brothers. Principal Toombs says, "You all know me as Principal Toombs. I've been the Principal here for the past ten years." The audience collectively gasps. Principal Toombs continues to say, "I've upheld a sacred ancient doctrine that dictates the type of dreams that come true. They must be happy, cheery, joyful, must be positive and fun filled." Mrs. TwoDreams says, "That's right!" Principal Toombs clears his throat and keeps saying, "Yes well, on Monday I have to take Simon Dreamlee in front of the parliamentary committee to have his latest dream coming true banned because it is dramatic, negative and not within the standards of Dreamville's ancient doctrine. I need every member of this town's support to stop his dream from coming true." Miss LossDream quickly gets on the stage with her own hovering microphone and says, "Don't listen to him. He's just jealous of Simon's dreams potential. On Monday, you'll embrace Simon's dream coming true. We live in Dreamville where dreams become true Principal Toombs." The musically inclined dreamers all cheer for Miss LossDream. Principal Toombs snorts like a bull and gets off the stage.

Pushing people out of his way, Principal Toombs storms out of the festival screaming, "Get out of my way. Out... Get out of my way." He walks back to his hover car and hovers in the direction of his house. Everyone at the summer festivities are quietly shocked at his appearance until Mayor Alldream says, "Happy, happy, everyone back to summer festivities! The chocolate soufflé is about to be served for supper! Let's go everyone!" The Dreamvillians collectively cheer. They all enter into the supper section lined with hundreds of tables with stainless steel tops. The festivities continue with the serving of the soufflé. The musically inclined dreamers all sit at the same table. "Hmm... This is so good!" says Jilla. Almont says, "I agree. This is the best chef Dreamchef has ever made for the festival. The coco must be extra productive this past summer." Jilla says, "Yeah it's too bad that the whole town has to start the new summer season with a parliamentary debate about your dream Simon. Personally, I love your dream and I can't wait for you to dream up the sequel with the answer and the happy ending." Simon says, "Yes, well, that's the problem. What if I don't dream of the happy ending? What if Principal Toombs is right and he finally has found a loop hole to stop our dreams from coming true? If he wins on Monday, there's no telling what length he'll go to, to stop anyone's dream from coming true. I'm worried." Almont says, "That's it." Simon says, "What's it." Almont says, "We find a loop hole to counter Principal Toombs loophole." Simon says, "And how do you suggest we do that?" Jilla says, "I don't play at the festival tomorrow and neither do you Simon. Maybe we could meet and research the ancient doctrine, read it and hope for the best." Simon says, "That sounds like a good plan to me. Come to my house at 10:00. My parents should be gone by then." Jilla says, "It's a date, uh, to research of course. Well I have to go; my mother's waving at me over there. Bye." Almont says, "Bye Jilla." Simon says, "Bye Jilla." Almont takes a bite of his soufflé and says, "Hmm... It really is a good soufflé!" Simon says, "Yeah it is."

Still sitting at the table, Mrs. Dreamlee walks up to Almont and Simon who are now quietly observing the science dreamers gadgets and says, "Simon, sweetheart, it's time to go home." Simon says, "But dad's still overseeing the science dreamer's inventions." His mother says, "Oh no they're done too. Your father will meet us at the hover car. Come now." Almont's mother comes up to Almont and says, "Yeah I agree with Simon's mom, it's time to go home Almont. Come along now." They both get up and Almont says, "See you Monday Simon." Simon says, "See you." Simon walks with his mother to the hover car. His father's already inside the hover car and they climb in too. They hover home in silence. Once in the hover way of their home, his father parks the car, they get out and together, they walk inside their house. Mrs. Dreamlee screams, "We've been robbed. Who in Dreamville would rob us? Everyone already dreams up what they want." Simon and his father look around the house that has been ransacked. Mr. Dreamlee says, "Whatever they were looking for, they didn't find it here because they didn't take anything." Mr. Dreamlee immediately makes a virtual call to the Dreamville dream squad to report the break and enter. He says, "Yes they ransacked the whole house but nothing was stolen." The Dream squad chief says, "That's odd now isn't it." Mr. Dreamlee says, "Yes it's odd. Who in Dreamville would do such a thing?" Simon tugs on his father's shirt and says, "Principal Toombs." Simon's father says, "My son thinks that maybe Principal Toombs did this. He did pull quite a scene today at the summer festival." The Dream squad chief says, "Yes, he would have been better off not going and that scene does make him the prime suspect. I'll send over the Dream investigators. Bye." Simon's father says, "Bye." They quietly sit on the couch waiting for them to arrive. Simon breaks the silence and says, "Strange, he didn't steal any technology or anything for that matter. I wonder what he thought he'd find here."

They hear a knock at the door. Mr. Dreamlee answers the door and welcomes in the Dream investigators. He says, "Come in officers, investigators as you can see the whole house, all the rooms are the crime scene." The dream squad chief says, "There hasn't been a crime in Dreamville in near ten years." Simon's intrigued by that comment and asks, "What kind of crime happened ten years ago?" The Dream squad chief replies, "Well son, we don't talk about it and it really doesn't concern you now. Run along and create your music." Simon sits on the couch as the investigators gather evidence. Simon whispers, "What are you adults hiding?" The dream squad chief comes down the stairs and says, "We have bad news for you Mr. and Mrs. Dreamlee. The prime suspect has a solid alibi that can be confirmed by five different Dreamvillians. It turns out after his verbal attack on your son he went straight to the Dreamville Giant Grocer by the Dreamville mall and spent the rest of the day pacing up and down the aisles. He only just now purchased the new dream catcher. Great invention by the way that last invention of yours, Mr. Dreamlee." Mr. Dreamlee says, "Oh yeah, it was a simple idea really." Mrs. Dreamlee interrupts and says, "Uh honey." Mr. Dreamlee says, "Ah yeah, it's a shame he isn't the robber but then I have no idea who it could be. We have no enemies a part from him that I'm aware of." The Chief says, "Well it's a filed case and my men and I will be on the lookout. So I'll see you. Sweet Dreams." Mr. Dreamlee says, "Sweet Dreams." Like that, the police were all gone. Mrs. Dreamlee turns around and says, "Look at this place. Look at the white powder everywhere. Amazing there still isn't a better way to find finger prints." She claps her hands three times and out of a closet in the laundry room, three house cleaning robots start cleaning the whole house. Simon sits and watches the robots, they were done in fifteen minutes and they went back into the laundry room closet. Simon's mom says, "That was one of your grandfather's inventions." She looks at Simon and says "Well we better go to bed. It's late and tomorrow's another summer festival day for your father and me. Go to bed Simon and sweet dreams son." Simon's father says, "Sweet Dreams son." Simon gets up from the couch and starts going upstairs. He turns around and sees his parents didn't wait for him to say sweet dreams back to them. Curious, he sneaks down the stairs to try and listen in on their conversation while they sit at the kitchen table.

Sitting around the kitchen table, Simon hears his father say, "Can it be true. Do you think it's going to happen again?" Simon's mother says, "We can't allow it to happen again. You need to find out how it's being done or how it was done ten years ago." Simon's dad says, "Yes but we never found any evidence then either. We still have nothing to work with." Simon's mother says, "Oh what's going to happen?" Simon's dad replies, "I don't know dear. I honestly don't know." They hug each other and Simon starts to go upstairs. He goes into his bedroom and sits on his bed. Simon whispers, "Whatever happened in Dreamville ten years ago must have been terrible." Simon's dog, Boomboom Booya, barks at him and Simon hushes him. He hears his parents coming up the stairs. He quickly attaches his dream catcher to his head, places his hands under his head and onto the pillow. Mr. and Mrs. Dreamlee poke their heads in his room and convinced he's asleep, they close his door. Simon sits up and detaches the dream catcher from his head. He listens at his door to hear his parents go to sleep. He opens his bedroom door and goes up to the attic. Simon whispers, "I'm going to spy on Principal Toombs all night if I have to." He peers out through his telescope and sees the darkness that surrounds Principal Toombs house. He's not satisfied with his view, he decides to go downstairs and get his hover bike.

Once outside, he gets on his hover bike and hovers up the hill to Principal Toombs scary, gloomy, dark, decrepit, run down, gargoyle decorated house. He parks his hover bike at the corner of the black fence and tip-toes through the tall grass to a window. He can't see anything. The window and all the windows are painted black. Walking around the house to the far side, he spots a stream of light coming out of the house through a hole in the wood side board. He chances it and looks inside. He's shocked by what he observes. He sees Principal Toombs crying in his black chair with the dream catcher attached to his head. Simon films him with his virtual communicator. He films the object on his head. On top of his head he's fastened some sort of primitive foil helmet with even more primitive antennas. Simon hears Principal Toombs mumble through his tears, "Why, why has this happened to me and only me? Why must I be alone in my suffering?" Outside, Simon's disturbed by a rat nibbling on his shoelace. Suddenly, he hears a loud crash. He looks inside and sees the dream catcher broken on the floor. Principal Toombs smashed it to pieces. Simon decides it's time for him to leave. He doesn't know where Principal Toombs is and he doesn't want to get caught. He pulls his laces out of the rat's mouth and tip toes around the yard passing by the Gargoyles and dead plants. He gets to his hover bike, pulls a snake off of it and kicks the multiple other snakes away from him and gets on his hover bike. He hovers quickly down the hill and to his house. He parks his hover bike and runs inside. Once inside, he locks the door, runs upstairs and slowly closes his bedroom door. He climbs into bed and stares at his ceiling trying to figure out what he just witnessed and heard. Simon whispers, "Principal Toombs crying. I've got to tell Almont." He sends a virtual message marked private to Almont. He attaches his dream catcher to his head and falls asleep instantly.

Fast asleep in his comfy and cozy bed, Simon's dream begins darkly. There's no sounds, no music, no singing, no dancing, not even faint voices in the distance, there's nothing for a long time. All of a sudden, a child dancer dressed in white appears out of nowhere. The child dances in the darkness on the stage. This isn't the oddest part of Simon's dream. The oddest part, the child has a key around his neck. Suddenly, Simon's dream fills with another verse and musical section after the dark ending.

R. E. Brémaud

The man, enduring
Years of suffering,
A Child,
Holds the key,
To release him
From his
Agonizing
Pain,
This child doesn't yet,
Know the solution
He possesses.
The child
Will be his freedom,
To start
Living again…

At the end of his dream, the lone boy stands in the middle of the stage. From above, a single ray of light streams right down onto him. Finally, more importantly, his dream ends on a more upbeat musical note.

Chapter Five – The Ancient Doctrine of Dreamville

The next day, Sunday Morning, Frankie Noodles wakes him up by purring in his face. "Purr, purr, purr… purr." He looks at the time and exclaims, "My parents let me sleep in until ten AM." He forgets to detach the dream catcher from his head when he tries to leave his room to answer the doorbell. He gets yanked back to his bed to discover his dream catcher's wrapped around his bedpost, he detaches it from his head, puts this personal computer chip sized computer in his jean pocket, and he quickly runs out of his room down the stairs to the front door to answer the doorbell. Simon says, "Hey Jilla. Thanks for coming." Jilla smiles and messes his hair with her hand. Jilla says, "Happy Sunday! Bed head hey, I guess you're just getting up." Simon says, "Ha, yeah. I slept in but I'm up now." She walks inside Simon's house and looks around. She says, "Nice house. I've always wondered what the inside of a fashion dreamer's house would be like. Hmm, it's glamorous!" Simon smiles and pets his dog. Jilla starts petting him too and says, "So where should we do this thing?" Simon says, "In the attic. We'll have more privacy there and if my parents come home we won't get caught researching the doctrine." Jilla replies, "Alright, let's go." They walk upstairs to the attic.

Once they're in the attic, they set up their folding computers. Jilla looks around and asks, "Who's the star gazer?" Simon says, "Oh I dabble in star gazing. If I didn't dream about music I'd study astronomy." Jilla says, "Huh, I guess you have a little of your father and grandfather in you after all." Simon says, "I guess. Well what do we type to bring up this doctrine?" Jilla says, "I'll try parliamentary doctrines and you try ancient doctrine." Simon says, "Okay I'll do that." As the hours pass by, they read page after page of the documents. Jilla explains, "These four documents explain how to organize the parliament." Simon says, "These three documents explain what each titled parliamentary member's job encompasses." Jilla says, "These two talk about how to form new laws." Simon says, "Two in the afternoon, we still haven't found anything feasible and useable to defend my dream." Jilla says, "Nothing yet. I'm beginning to think this isn't going to benefit us much unless we decide to pursue politics." Simon sighs and says, "Wait I found it. I typed in Dreamville's sacred ancient doctrine. Here it is!" Jilla quickly types this in her computer and the doctrine pops up before her eyes. They look at each other and give each other a high five. Jilla exclaims, "Quick start reading to find the loop hole you need to win your case." They start reading, one hour goes by, another hour goes by and finally Jilla says, "Listen to this. According to ancient law established centuries ago, in year one, it was proclaimed that Dreamville's exact location will always remain and is to be kept a secret from outsiders. Contact with outsiders will always be forbidden. Dreamvillians will earn their living from their dreams coming true but only the head dreamer will be allowed to venture out of the city to sell their products. A Non-Dreamvillian will not be allowed to enter the city or work in any capacity within the city walls." Jilla pauses for a moment and says, "Walls? What walls?" Simon says, "That's not what concerns me right now. Miss DreamNot doesn't live in Dreamville." Jilla asks, "How do you know?" Simon replies, "Almont and I followed her to her shack in the outer woods. She lives in the shack." Jilla says, "She's a Dreamvillian though Simon. She's my mom's fourth cousin. I guess that makes her my fifth cousin." Simon says, "Huh, that's interesting. Well keep reading." Their reading's interrupted when they hear Simon's parents hover into the hover way of the house. Simon says, "Quick fold up your computer. We have to get to the back door." Without hesitating, Jilla swiftly folds her computer, slips it in her pocket and they run downstairs. Jilla asks, "Why are we hiding the fact that we're researching this document anyway?" Simon replies, "Because the adults are hiding something." Jilla goes out the back door just as Simon's parents come in the front door.

Simon's mom says, "Simon we're home son!" Simon's father says, "I brought you a gadget." Simon walks out of the kitchen and smiles at them. His dad pats his head and says, "Rino DreamScifi's invention to temporarily filter or stop your dreams has been proven to work without harming anyone. I have here two of his dream stoppers. I'm giving one to you and I'm taking the other one to work. I'll patent it and market it for him. He's going to be a rich fourteen year old teenager." Simon says, "That's great dad! Thanks. I'll be in the attic." Mrs. Dreamlee says, "Now son aren't you hungry?" Simon says, "No, not really. Thanks anyway. I'll be in the attic." They watch Simon go upstairs to the attic. Mr. Dreamlee says, "He's alright dear. He's just nervous for tomorrow morning. That's all." Mrs. Dreamlee says, "You're probably right dear. Well it's suppertime." They go into the kitchen and Mrs. Dreamlee says, "Lemon meringue pie and freshly squeezed pink lemonade will taste scrumptious together!"

Back in the attic, Simon contacts Jilla with his virtual communicator. Simon says, "Jilla respond." Jilla replies, "Jilla responding." Simon says, "Wait I'll get Almont on three way virtual wave. Almont says, "Simon responding." Simon says, "Hey Almont! How was your day?" Almont says, "Uneventful. Did you guys find anything?" Jilla says, "Hey Almont." Almont says, "Oh hey Jilla." Simon says, "Okay back to business." Jilla says, "Right, back to business." Simon says, "I'll read a portion of the doctrine out loud to both of you. It says here that Dreamville has one purpose. The purposes, to enhance, entertain, better the imaginations and elevate the standards of living of the outsiders. Dreamvillians must concur to one notion and one type of dream. All dreams must fall under one of the following purposeful categories at all times, be positive, cheery, light hearted, love filled, fun, enthusiastic, endearing, embraceable, memorable, catchy, hummable, danceable, romantic, helpful, useable and most importantly they cannot be negative, dramatic, or possess dark messages." Jilla finishes the paragraph, "At all times the lyrics must have positive messages. Due to the power that Dreamvillians have over the world when their dreams become true leads this council of Dreamville to establish this as their final decision. Therefore, on this day the law is put forth and is binding to all Dreamvillians and their descendants for eternity." They're all startled when they hear Jilla's mother calling her to bed. Jilla's mom says, "Jilla dear go to bed." Jilla says, "Yes mom." Simon says, "Sweet dreams Jilla." Almont says, "Sweet dreams Jilla." Jilla says, "Sweet dreams guys and I'm sorry we didn't find what you needed Simon." Jilla signs out and it's now a two way virtual screen between Simon and Almont. Simon says, "I'm going to stay up all night. I'm going to read this document page by page." Almont says, "Good luck Simon. Oh and by the way I got your virtual video of Principal Toombs in his house. I saw it with my own eyes and yet I still can't believe he was crying." Simon says, "I know. I don't quite understand it either." Almont's mom yells, "Almont dear. Go to bed. Sweet dreams son." Almont looks at Simon through the virtual screen. Simon says, "I'll be okay Almont. Sweet dreams." Almont says, "Sorry. Sweet dreams to you too." Almont signs out of the virtual screen and Simon turns off his virtual communicator. Alone to read the document, Simon sighs and keeps reading. He whispers as he reads, "Any Dreamvillian's dream or multiple Dreamvillians dreams do not meet the standards and criteria put forth in this document justifies the implication of the automatic application of the law to ban the dream or dreams. This law will be, at all times, strongly enforced. Once a dream is banned, it's banned forever." Simon sighs and puts his head in his hands. He hears his mother say, "Simon go to bed dear. Sweet dreams." Simon looks up; he's tired and has ten more pages to read. He goes to his room and closes the door. Mr. Dreamlee opens the door and pokes his head in his room. He says, "Son, I want to update you that Principal Toombs has definitely been ruled out as a suspect for the break and enter because it turns out someone was lurking around his house last night. The cops gathered foot prints outside his house and backyard. So with that said, son, good luck tomorrow. Sweet dreams son." Simon yawns and says, yeah sweet dreams dad." His father closes the door and Simon lies in bed with his arms behind his head staring at the ceiling. Simon whispers, "Great, like I don't already have enough to worry about. Now they'll match my shoe prints to the prints around Principal Toombs house. I'm only twelve what more could happen to me? What's next?" He hears his parents go into their bedroom and shut their door. Yawning some more, tired, eyes aching, he gets up and tip toes to his door. He slowly opens the door and tip toes to the attic. Accidently, he steps on his Frankie Noodles tail, his cat screeches. "MEOW…" Simon hushes her, "Shush!"

Back in the attic at midnight, Simon keeps reading from where he left off. He whispers, "Okay I've found one flaw in this document so far. They list more than one purpose. What other possible flaws and maybe a loophole in my favor can I find?" His eyes grow heavy making it difficult for him to keep his eyes open. He whispers, "I need some sugar." He tip toes downstairs and cuts a piece of the lemon meringue pie and eats the entire remaining pie from the pie dish. He brings the single piece of pie with him upstairs. But before he makes it upstairs he hears a loud crash outside. He runs to the back door and hears someone scurrying away but can't make out anything. He whispers, "I'm not chancing going outside, besides, right now, I've got something more important to worry about and solve by tomorrow morning." With his original mission in mind, he tip toes upstairs to the attic and attempts to read some more. Still heavy eyed and drowsy, he eats the single piece of pie. He whispers, "Okay… Back to business, where was I?" Momentarily, Simon's eyes grow heavy and he falls to sleep. His face falls on the computer screen and he's jolted awake. He whispers, "I need some restricted to adult only food to help me stay awake." He tip toes back downstairs and opens the cupboard, he takes out caffeinated candy, he swallows about a dozen and within seconds he feels awake. Simon tip-toes back upstairs to the attic. He starts to read in a very soft, very low whisper, "Okay here I was. Banned forever... " He hears the birds chirping and the sunlight starts to brightly light the attic. He spent so much time going up and down the stairs and trying to stay awake that he didn't get to read any further. He hears his parent's bedroom door open. He whispers, "Okay before I get busted. We as council have established one road in and out of Dreamville. This road will be forbidden to all Dreamvillians. Those who dare to travel down this road will suffer great death at the ferociously sharp teeth of the untamable wild animals that inhabit the wall of forest, even though they were all brought there to protect the residence of Dreamville from outside harm, or, and perhaps death at the hands of one of the outsiders. Lastly, regarding this issue and due to this potential threat, Dreamvillians are banned from living in the forest. Hum... Banned, this means Miss DreamNot's breaking the law." Simon's mother walks in the attic and says, "Simon, you must be nervous for this parliamentary meeting today huh? Especially, to already be up before your dad and me." Simon turns around and hides his computer screen with his body. Simon says, "Yeah, nervous. I am worried that's for sure mom." Mr. Dreamlee yells from the second floor, "Is he up there dear?" Mrs. Dreamlee replies, "Yes dear, he's up here." She smiles at Simon and holds out her hand. Simon takes her hand and they walk out of the attic. He looks back at his computer screen and wonders what he missed in the ancient document. They walk downstairs and into the kitchen. Simon's mom says, "We'll eat a good breakfast before going to your trial that way whatever the outcome you have a belly full of good food." She sits him at the kitchen table across from his father and places a bowl of chocolate ice cream with fresh strawberries in front of him. She hands him a spoon and Simon eats. Silence fills the room until Mr. Dreamlee says, "Now son no matter what happens today, I'm proud of your dream. Also, I don't want you to be scared of the virtual news clown broadcasters that are going to be everywhere. They look like clowns. My advice, do not answer any of their questions. You just walk right by them." Simon finishes his breakfast and says, "That's great advice dad. Truly, thanks." The hovering virtual digital clock rings to indicate it's eight AM. Mr. Dreamlee says, "We better get to the parliament building. I don't want to be late. Simon sighs and says, "I have one thing I need to do before we leave." He quickly gets up before his parents can respond and runs up to the attic. He rereads the section about dreams. He whispers, "I know there's got to be something here." His virtual communicator goes on and the virtual three way screen pops up both Almont and Jilla are on the virtual three way wave. Jilla says, "Anything Simon?" Simon says, "Nothing." Almont says, "Simon get to your hearing and Jilla and I will keep reading. Show us where you are in the document." Simon links them to the section of the document he's reading via virtual document transfer. Almont and Jilla say at the same time, "Got it." Simon replies, "Okay I'm gone." He shuts off his virtual communicator and puts it in his pocket. He runs downstairs just as his mother yells, "Simon, we have to go to avoid the hover jam." Face to face with his mother, Simon gets an earful. She grabs his hand, they rush out to the hover car, they climb inside and Mr. Dreamlee starts hovering towards the hover way.

On the hover way, to his relief, Simon sees Principal Toombs is not that much ahead of them. Simon's mother says, "Look there's Principal Toombs. We'll wave at him as we drive by him." Mr. Dreamlee says, "Poor guy. He's in the wrong hover lane. He's the one that's going to be late this morning." Mrs. and Mr. Dreamlee wave at him as they hover by his hover car. Principal Toombs yells, "This doesn't mean you've won Simon." Simon's dad looks in his rearview mirror and says, "Why in all of Dreamville would he yell that. That doesn't even make any sense to be yelling that now. After the trial maybe, if he loses, but why now. What a strange man." Mrs. Dreamlee says, "And he's getting stranger." They hover into the parliament building and park in the parkade for hover cars. They get out of the hover car. A Dreamville dream media team hovers up in their hover van. The reporter with the face of a clown leans out the window and asks, "Simon, how does it feel to stir up so much controversy over one silly little dream?" Simon and his parents keep looking forward and walk right into the parliamentary building and into a barrage of media clown reporters from all the virtual stations. Mr. Dreamlee pushes their way through the frenzy and into the hearing room. As they enter they can hear Principal Toombs making comments to the clown reporters. He says, "Simon's dream is not only inappropriate, it's completely against the ancient doctrine that we Dreamvillians honor, respect and uphold without variation. I will destroy his dream from becoming true."

In the hearing room, Simon goes to the front of the room and takes his designated seat. Principle Toombs enters and takes his designated seat right beside Simon. Their seats are located in front and face the parliamentary judge. The members of the parliamentary committee sit on either side of the judge. To the judge's left Mayor Alldream and his assistant and to the judge's right is the only person who's allowed to leave Dreamville to market their products. Simon looks back, he sees all his classmates, his parents and Miss LossDream. To his disappointment, he doesn't see Almont or Jilla anywhere. Simon's losing faith in his ability to win his case. He turns to look at Principal Toombs and wonders how this can be the same man he saw crying the other night. How can a man like that want to destroy his dream from coming true? Simon realizes he has to melt his heart somehow. The question is; how to achieve the impossible? Simon gets an idea and walks up to the judge and says, "Judge I know we haven't begun yet but in order for my case to be fairly trialed I need to submit the final verses to my dream." The judge looks down on Simon and says, "Very well give me your hand held, computer chip sized computer." Simon passes him his hand held computer and the judge places it in the pod to download. Simon says, "Download to the judges files." The judge says, "Okay son. The download is complete. Here's your hand held computer. Now go get ready to be sworn in for your trial." Simon says, "Thank you judge." Simon walks back to his seat and sits down. Principal Toombs whispers, "Whatever trick you're up to Simon, the judge will catch you." Simon whispers, "I'm not up to anything sir." The Judge says, "All rise for me. Now everyone may be seated once I have sat down." He sits and everyone sits as well. The judge says, "Simon Dreamlee approach the bench." Simon approaches the bench and puts his hand on the book titled; The Sacred Ancient Doctrine. The judge says, "Simon Dreamlee, do you swear to obey the laws of Dreamville and everything that the ancients wrote in the doctrine that guides us to this very day?" Simon replies, "I do swear to it." The judge says, "You may be seated. Principal Toombs you may approach the bench." Principal Toombs approaches the bench but first he purposefully trips Simon before he can reach his seat. Simon gets up, brushes himself off and sits in the chair. The judge says, "Principal Toombs, do you swear to obey the laws of Dreamville and everything that the ancients wrote in the doctrine that guides us to this very day?" Principal Toombs replies, "I do swear to it." The judge says, "You may be seated." Everyone waits for him to sit in his chair. The judge says, "Esteemed members of the parliamentary committee, Mayor Alldream, Mrs. DreamMarketer and everyone who's attending this hearing today, in light of some new evidence that has been submitted moments ago, I'm obligated to call a brief recess to review this before passing a fair judgement. You may all remain seated. I shall be back." The judge rises and everyone rises with him, he winks at Simon and enters into his chambers. Everyone sits down and whispers fill the acoustics of the room. Desperately, Simon looks around to see if Almont and Jilla made it to the trial. He checks his virtual communicator messaging service and the display indicates no messages. Simon whispers, "I can't believe that there's no loop hole in the ancient doctrine to help me right now." Principal Toombs whispers, "Believe it kid. Life is not a dream." The judge's chamber door slowly opens. A hush fills the room. Everyone stands up while the judge walks to his chair and everyone sits when he sits in his chair. He looks at Principal Toombs and then at Simon. The judge's looking sternly at the two of them and he's unreadable. Principal Toombs looks conniving and manipulative. Finally, the judge says, "Let the trial begin." The judge raises his gavel and taps it on his bench.

Chapter Six – Simon's On Trial

Dead silence fills the hearing room with not a sound, not even a breeze whistling anywhere. Simon sits silently looking forward waiting for the judge to ask questions. The judge just stares blankly at the two of them for fifteen minutes. The ancient grandfather clock with its ancient, old fashioned face ticks loudly. "Tick, Tock, Tick, Tock." The parliament members copy how the judge's acting. When suddenly Simon's virtual communicator sounds off to indicate he has a message. Simon's eyes get large as he looks at the judge's lack of facial expression and softly says, "Sorry, I'll just turn this off." But before he does, he quickly reads the message from Almont. He reads with his inner, internal voice, "Simon so far Jilla and I haven't come across any loop hole that can help your case. We're paying close attention to the proceedings on the virtualvision just outside of the hearing room. At the same time, we're reading the rest of the document. So there's still hope. Hang in there. Remember your friends are supporting you no matter what the outcome. Peace." Simon puts his virtual communicator in his pocket and looks up at the judge. Despite the judge's glare at him, Simon's relieved that Almont and Jilla are at the trial with him. They may not be in the hearing room but they're still there in the parliament building waiting for him until the end of his trial. After another ten minutes of excruciating silence, the judge breaks his silence and says, "Principal Toombs you may present your case and evidence to the court." Principal Toombs stands up as straight as he can and walks to the middle of the floor before the bench and says, "Esteemed participants in this altogether very useful trial today I would like to simply present Simon's dream to everyone and let the dream speak for itself. Judge if you may, please press the play button." The judge says, "I will oblige." The judge presses the play button. Principal Toombs continues to say, "Before you today will play the dream that was submitted by Simon Dreamlee to Miss LossDream during her class for the musically inclined dreamers."

The oversized hovering screen plays the fifteen minute portion of Simon's dream that he, in fact, presented in class.

Fifteen minutes later, Principal Toombs begins to say, "As you can clearly see this dream does not fit the one purpose as per the ancient doctrine being not happy, not cheery, not positive, and doesn't even have a positive ending. His dream, without a doubt, is against the ancient doctrine. I will quote it." The judge interrupts, "That will not be necessary Principal Toombs. Everyone here has read the doctrine and we're well aware of the wording. Continue with your evidence." Principal Toombs continues to say, "My evidence, dear judge, is apparent with the simple fact that his dream's storyline describes a woman who's capable of destroying true love. Now how many of us want true love to be destroyed? None of us do and certainly, not I. Furthermore, the reason for this cruel act goes without explanation either. His Dream simply, without a doubt, verges on a nightmare. Now that, undeniably, is reason enough to ban and destroy his dream from coming true. After all, in Dreamville there's no place for nightmares. Is there? I ask you, is there place for nightmares in Dreamville? No there isn't. This has been the law since year one when the ancient esteemed members of parliament of those days fabricated our most sacred ancient doctrine of laws. We as members of this trial must uphold and obey these laws. Therefore, Simon's dream must be banned and destroyed before it infects our psyche. Thank you." Principal Toombs bows before the judge and waits for his response. The judge says, "You may rise and stand Principal Toombs." Principal Toombs rises and stands before the judge. The judge says, "You have made a clear cut case regarding the reasons you believe that Simon's dream must be banned. You have used the ancient doctrine to make a profoundly thought provoking case against an innocent child's dream. Evidently, your goal today is to destroy his dream's chance of coming true and you've based your argument on what you see as the message of Simon's dream. Thank you. I turn to the members of parliament and ask them to raise their hands if they agree with Principal Toombs presentation." The judge signals to them to vote. Simon watches in dismay as one by one they all raise their hands to indicate they agree with Principal Toombs. All fifty-one members vote in favor of Principal Toombs. The audience gasps in disbelief at the result of the vote. The judge says, "Fifty-one members vote in your favor at this point of the trial Principal Toombs. That's every single member. Please take your seat." Principal Toombs turns around and smiles at Simon with his dirty yellow teeth. Principal Toombs looks out at the audience with conniving in his eyes and sits in his chair. The judge says, "There will be a brief recess while I confer with my members of parliament in my chambers. You may all remain seated." The judge rises and everyone rises. The committee follows the judge into his chambers and the door shuts. Everyone sits down and whispers fill the air once again. Principal Toombs leans towards Simon and whispers, "You're done for Simon. I will succeed at destroying your dream and I'm only beginning." Simon could smell his stinky breath and he covers his nose. Simon whispers back, "Could you face the other way? You're choking me with your disgusting breath." Principal Toombs loses his smile, glares at Simon and leans back in his chair.

Another fifteen minutes later, the committee comes out of the judge's chambers and they close the door. Everyone ceases their chattering but seeing that the judge did not come out of his chamber, they all start whispering again. Simon tries to make out what people are saying but with so many opinions, he can't clearly distinguish them in his head. Suddenly he feels a hand on his shoulder and he quickly turns around to see his father. Mr. Dreamlee says, "Hang in there son. You'll do fine just listen to your heart." He watches his father walk back to his seat, sit, and give him the thumbs up. Simon looks around for Almont and Jilla but they're still not in the hearing room. Everyone rises before Simon's eyes, Simon turns around and see's the judge waiting for him to rise. Simon rises out of his chair, the judge sits and everyone including Simon sits in their chairs. Principal Toombs sarcastically whispers, "You really know how to make an impression kid." Simon covers his nose again. The judge looks up at Principal Toombs and then at Simon. He looks out at the audience and says, "Principal Toombs presented an extremely compelling, convincing and factual case before the members of parliament and me, however, in all fairness, Simon's allotted a turn to defend his dream. Simon you may precede with your case." Simon rises from his chair and walks slowly to the center of the floor and bows before the judge. The judge says, "Bowing before me is not necessary Simon." Simon stands up and says, "Oh!" Simon looks at the members of parliament and back at the judge. The judge says, "I understand you're nervous Simon but don't waste your time." Simon says, "Oh of course. Um, judge if you could play my dream in its entirety with the appropriate ending. Please." The judge says, "I will do just that." The hover screen descends from the ceiling and his dream plays again with the ending he submitted.

Forty five minutes later, the audience claps and cheers. "Bravo, bravo! Encore!" The judge raises his gavel and taps it on his bench. He says,

"Order, order. I demand order in my courtroom." Everyone becomes quiet. The judge says, "Now please continue Simon." Simon nods his head and begins, "First, I'd like to thank the audience for their very positive reaction to my dream. This reaction alone, I think, indicates that my dream, in fact, is not at all against the ancient doctrine and does fit some of the many purposes of our dreams as Dreamvillians. Now, I know I may just have confused some of you but I have in fact read the doctrine myself and although it indicates that our dreams have one purpose, the doctrine goes on to list many purposes. My dream can be categorized under enhancing the imagination of everyone including the outsiders. My dream has true love in it, positivity in it, happiness in it, joy in it and it has a positive message in it as well. Of course, I'm sure the members of parliament and Principal Toombs are wondering; what is the positive message? Well before I answer this question, I'd like to address the negative portion of my dream. I believe my dream pushes the boundaries of the standards in a positive way. My dream's progressive, evolutionary and the future or futuristic because there's negativity with the third woman succeeding to accomplish her plot to destroy true love. My dream has a sense of intrigue and leaves the spectator wanting to know more, which allows me to address Principal Toombs concern that my dream may be a nightmare. If it were a nightmare no one would have been compelled to clap for my dream. Their reaction brings me to my final point, the appearance of the child in white with the mysterious key around his neck signifies a message to remain innocent and never lose hope and faith in true love returning. Therefore, my dream ends positively which is within the law of the ancient doctrine." Simon waits for the judge to react. The judge says, "Interesting argument Simon has presented before the members of parliament and me. I tend to agree with you Simon that there are some very good elements in your dream. Unfortunately, there's still the negative portion and the unanswered question of how she did it that has yet to be answered. Whether yes or no your dream's a nightmare, falls within the eye of the beholder. I'm faced with a very tough decision today Simon. I turn to my members of parliament and ask that they cast their votes. Show a raise of hands from those who agree with Simon's arguments." Simon looks at the members of parliament and none of them raise their hands. The audience gasps again in disbelief. The judge says, "Well Simon it appears that none of them agree with you. You may take your seat. I will be in my chamber reviewing both arguments and I will come back with my final verdict. You may all remain seated." The judge rises and everyone rises. He enters his chamber and closes the door behind him. Everyone sits and start to whisper. Simon returns to his seat while Principal Toombs smiles at him with victory written all over his face. Principal Toombs leans towards him and softly says, "I told you life is not a dream. Didn't I? Ha-ha." Simon covers his nose and pushes Principal Toombs face away from his face with his other hand and stomps on his foot. Simon whispers, "There's nothing you can do about that." Principal Toombs just holds his foot in his hand and glares at Simon.

The judge stays in his chamber for twenty-five minutes before coming out of his chamber. Finally, his door opens and everyone rises. He takes his seat and everyone sits. He sits silently looking at Principal Toombs and Simon. If a pin sized computer chip dropped from a new hand held computer it would sound like a wrecking ball destroying a building. Ten more minutes goes by and still the judge says nothing at all. Twenty more minutes go by and still the judge says nothing. After another thirty-two minutes, the judge says, "I've carefully reviewed both arguments. Both equally weigh against each other with valid, useable facts, points and explanations. Both have successfully implicated the sacred ancient doctrine in their presentations as well. I respect what Principal Toombs had to say regarding Simon's dream. But is it just an opinion based on an overreaction to Simon's story. Not necessarily. No one who's seen his dream can deny the definite negative elements in his dream. These elements can be interpreted differently as they have both indicated today. Principal Toombs reaction is to say that it's a nightmare where Simon says it's evolutionary and progressive. Simon even goes as far as to say his dream's futuristic. That, I question a little, however, with the submission of the actual ending, he makes another strong and valid point. His dream does end positively with the notion that hope and faith will rekindle true love but unfortunately for people who react like Principal Toombs this very same ending may still be garnered as negative because of the lack of explanation regarding how this third evil woman succeeds to break up two people who are so obviously in love and they do not end up back together, therefore, a negative ending. All of this evidence presented before me today makes my decision and judgement that much more difficult." The judge stops talking and silence fills the room again. He stares forward for another ten minutes. Suddenly, Simon's virtual communicator vibrates and Simon pulls it out of his pocket. He reads a message from Almont and Jilla. Simon barely gets to finish reading the message when the judge starts to speak again. The Judge says, "All of Dreamville's Dreamvillians will remember this day as a historical one. I rule in favor of Prince..." Simon yells, "No judge you can't." The judge says, "Well Simon, I most certainly can." Simon jumps up and down and says, "No you can't. There's a clause at the bottom of the final page of the ancient doctrine. It's in very fine print so you're going to need a looking glass." The judge picks up the book and turns to the final page. He pulls out his looking glass and begins to read. Simon says, "My friends found this clause on the virtual version we researched. It's been enlarged in the virtual version." The judge hushes him, "Shush." Principal Toombs says, "No way. Judge you were ruling in my favor because I'm right and your members of parliament agree with me too." The judge looks up and smiles at Simon. He says, "I'll read the clause. It states that if in such an event where a Dreamvillian's dream or multiple Dreamvillians dreams have an element or many elements of negativity but still end with hope and faith as the final message, the dream shall not be banned due to the potential for a sequel. The foregone conclusion of the sequel to the dream or dreams in question will explain the negative element or elements and will without a doubt end positively making the dream or dreams as per this doctrine not suited for banishment." The judge closes the book and listens to the audience as they erupt with cheers. Surprisingly, the parliament members also cheer for Simon too. The judge genuinely smiles at Simon and says, "I rule in favor of Mr. Simon Dreamlee and making his dream come true!" The judge raises his gavel and taps it on the bench. No one waits for the judge to rise as every person in the audience jumps up for joy and congratulate Simon's parents. The judge and the parliament members go into the judge's chambers and they shut the door.

Almont and Jilla force their way past the security guards into the hearing room and run down to Simon. Jilla hugs Simon and kisses him on the cheek. Simon blushes and says, "Thanks Jilla!" Jilla says, "Don't thank me. Almont found the clause." Simon turns to Almont, they high five each other. Simon says, "Thanks Almont!" Jilla's mom calls her to go home, "Jilla quickly now we have to get home." Jilla says, "Well I'll see you guys tomorrow at school." Simon says, "Yeah tomorrow." Almont says, "See you tomorrow Jilla." Simon shakes off and says, "Girl germs. Ha-ha." Almont laughs too. Almont says, "Oh my parents are waving at me to go. I'll see you tomorrow Simon. Get some sleep tonight. Sweet dreams." Simon says, "Sweet dreams Almont." Mr. and Mrs. Dreamlee walk up to their son with giant smiles. His father says, "You did well today son. Now we use the same strategy to get to the hover car and home. Do not talk to the media clowns." Simon says, "Okay dad!" Mr. Dreamlee leads the way pushing the media clowns out of the way. They can hear Principal Toombs banging and yelling at the judge's chamber door, "No, no, no, I'm right. I'm right. Simon's dream must be destroyed." They witness the guards escorting Principal Toombs away from the door, past them and out of the parliament building to his hover car before they make it to their hover car. Just before reaching the hover car they get stopped by a clown reporter who asks, "Simon how does it feel to make history today in Dreamville?" Simon quickly replies, "It feels like an amazingly cool accomplishment. I think many Dreamvillians will now look forward to the future." He gets in his parents hover car and they hover onto the hover way where people honk, flash signs saying we heart Simon Dreamlee and wave at them as they hover by on their way home.

While still hovering home, Mr. Dreamlee asks, "Why so silent son?" Simon replies, "I'm just in awe and incredibly tired." Mrs. Dreamlee says, "Yeah I guess when you stay up all night reading the sacred ancient doctrine." Simon smiles at his parents. They hover up their hover way driveway, into their garage and dock in the solar paneled recharger. Simon gets out and walks in the house. He walks straight upstairs to his room and lies on his bed with his arms behind his head. His parents poke their heads in his room and say simultaneously, "Sweet Dreams son." Simon says, "Sweet Dreams!" Simon attaches his dream catcher to his head and once his head touches the pillow he automatically falls asleep. His parents close the door to his bedroom and they go to sleep too.

Snug, comfy, warm, tucked under his covers, Simon dreams up note after note of a simple little song with lyrics to match his new melody.

Dream Dreamvillian Dream.
There was a boy,
Dreamed,
A dream,
All who viewed it cheered.
All cheered but one.
Heartless,
This one tried to destroy
This boy's dream
But as dreams would go,
He didn't
Stop the boy's dream
From coming

R. E. Brémaud

> True.
> Dream Dreamvillian Dream.
> Dreams do come
> True.

Simon sleeps soundly throughout the night with this lovely, short, victory tune floating through his dream.

Chapter Seven – Everything's Seemingly Back to Normal

Tuesday Morning, Simon wakes up like he does every morning but this morning he's in a particularly happier mood than usual. He says to his dog, Boomboom Booya, "Happy Tuesday pal. I, Simon Dreamlee, made history yesterday. I've made it possible to have negative elements in our dreams, more importantly, my dreams. Dreamvillians are free to dream about whatever they dream and their dreams will come true." Boomboom Booya barks, "Woof, woof, woof!" Simon sits up and pets his dog. He detaches his dream catcher and reviews his new song. He says, "Hmm, catchy." He stands up and opens his bedroom door. He walks downstairs and into the kitchen where his parents are watching the virtual newscast. The clown reporter says, "It's another dreamy day in Dreamville. The sky's blue, the sun's brightly and dreamily shining and there's not a cloud in the sky. In fact, does anyone in Dreamville even know what clouds resemble? I don't! Ha-ha! Well have a dreamy, happy Tuesday. We all know one little boy that definitely will. Simon Dreamlee successfully defended his dream yesterday during his parliamentary hearing and the verdict; his dream will come true. A dreamy congratulations to you Simon." Mr. Dreamlee turns off the virtual news and says, "Happy Tuesday son. You made the news on every news wave." Simon replies, "Wow, that's great. I'm happy to have advanced our views about dreams coming true." Mrs. Dreamlee says, "Yes well. Today, everything's back to normal and you have to get to school." Simon says, "Oh right. Let's go then. I'll grab a raspberry cupcake from the fridge for lunch and a banana for breakfast." Mr. Dreamlee says, "Let's get in the hover car." Simon replies, "Nah, thanks anyway but I like to take my hover bike. Bye mom. Bye dad." Simon goes out the back door and gets on his hover bike. He starts to hover stilly in the air.

Still in a stand still hover, Simon looks at Principal Toombs house and watches as his car hovers down the hill towards Dreamtrue School. Simon whispers, "I've made quite an enemy yesterday. There's no telling what Principal Toombs might try to do for revenge." Simon starts to hover up to the intersection and Almont hovers up on his new hover board. Almont says, "Happy Tuesday! I hope you got some sleep." Simon smiles, "Happy Tuesday and yes I got a really good night's rest last night. I went to sleep as soon as I got home. Wicked hover board!" They start hovering towards the school. Mrs. Dreammore and Mrs. LandDream say, "Congratulations Simon. I can't wait to see your dream in theatres." Simon replies, "Thank you, thank you." Mr. BottomDream says, "Good job chap." Simon replies, "Thanks Mr. BottomDream. See you at the theatre." Almont says, "Well I guess everything's back to normal!" Simon says, "For now, but I was thinking that Principal Toombs isn't going to go down without a fight. He'll try exacting his revenge. I just have to be on the lookout." Almont says, "You think so. I thought he might start to think you're untouchable now." They hover into the hover bike parkade and park their hovering contraptions. Simon says, "I don't think so. He's evil and evil doesn't ever rest." Almont and Simon get off of their hover bikes and walk up the sidewalk to the front door. Principal Toombs stands there glaring at them as they walk in the front door. Once in the corridor, Almont says, "Well we managed to walk in the school without him stopping us to make ridiculous accusations. That's got to be a bonus for us." They give each other a high five. They reach the entry door to the theatre room and enter.

They walk to their desks, sit and wash their hands with hand sanitizer while they wait for Miss LossDream to start the class. In the meantime, Simon uploads a copy of his dream's ending from his computer chip sized hand held computer to Miss LossDream's files. He says, "Upload to Miss LossDream's files." She stands in front of the class, waits for everyone to stop talking and says, "Yesterday was a tremendous victory for musically inclined dreamers as well as the dreamers of the other disciplines. It's a day that will definitely be recorded in the Dreamville history book and we all have Simon Dreamlee to thank!" Miss Dreamlee starts to clap her hands and the whole class start to clap their hands too. Miss Dreamlee blows him a kiss and says, "Now class, with all the commotion over, it's time to get back to business. This afternoon we will finalize Simon's dream coming true with the addition of his ending. So everyone practice, practice, practice until opening night and filming. Your dream Simon is going to be made into a movie. Bravo Simon! Bravo!" The class claps their hands again.

Simon nods his head, smiles and says, "Thank you!" Miss LossDream continues to say, "This morning we will be viewing the new dreams of your classmates. We'll start with you Almont Alldream." Almont clears his throat, takes a big gulp and says, "Okay Miss LossDream." He presses play and his dream plays on the large screen for the whole class.

The images of animated chess board pieces form in front of everyone's eyes. They're playing a game of chess. It's a unique, quirky and fun dream filled with upbeat music and rhythms. Drums, mandolins, keyboards, guitars and a variety of flutes make up the instruments that carry his dreamed up composition. The lyrics begin to be sung.

Computer age,
Indeed,
But there's always time
For
The ancient game of...
What's that?
Chessboard,
Save the King,
Protect the Queen,
Bishop move here,
Castle goes there,
Oh,
Oh,
Oh,
The White King wins!
Computer age,
So what!
Make time for
An ancient game of
Chess,
Oh,
Oh,
Oh,
An ancient game of
Chess,
Oh,
Oh,
Oh.

Simon taps Almont on the shoulder and says, "That was really cool Almont." Almont turns around and says, "Thanks Simon." The class claps their hands and Miss LossDream says, "Well done Almont. That was fun, upbeat and very cute." Almont replies, "Thank you Miss LossDream." Miss LossDream asks, "Who wants to share their dream next?" Jilla puts up her hand. Miss LossDream smiles and says, "Okay Jilla MusiDream your up." Jilla presses play and her dream appears on the big screen. Her dream's light and airy like a fairy tale. There' angels fluttering around everywhere and flowers fill the screen. The music's played by a single harp. The lyrics are fluffy and sweet like candy.

Angel,
Oh angel,
Angel,
Oh angel,
You flutter here and there,
Your goodness
Shining down on us
Angel,
Oh angel,
Angel,
Oh angel,
You spread your fluffy white wings,
Your kindness
Enveloping us,
Angel,
Oh angel,
Angel,
Oh angel,
Today,
Come and say hello to me.
Oh Angel!

Simon sends a virtual silent message to Jilla telling her, her songs captivating. Miss LossDream says, "Beautiful song Jilla! That's very romantic!" The class claps their hands for Jilla and she says, "Thanks everyone!" Jilla smiles at Simon and he blushes. Miss LossDream says, "Now who wants to be next Oh... the lunch bell. Submit your dreams and I'll have them back to you this afternoon with your ratings. Oh yes Almont you get four stars out of five and Jilla you get four and a half stars out of five." Almont turns to Simon and says, "Four stars. Not too bad. Cool!" Jilla walks up to them and asks, "Do you guys want to have lunch with me?" Almont stands up and says, "Yeah sure, come and join us." Simon smiles, "We'd be delighted, besides, I have things to talk to you about." They all go to the lunchroom without being stopped by Principal Toombs. Simon looks in the Principal's office as they walk by and he sees Miss DreamNot sitting in her chair sorting more obsolete computer chips into boxes. Simon says, "That's odd." Jilla says, "What's odd?" They stop in front of the door and look at Miss DreamNot. Miss DreamNot gets up and says, "Nosy, good for nothing kids." She slams the door shut. Simon says, "That's odd. Why does she hang onto all those obsolete computer chips instead of recycling them?" They all look at each and continue to the lunchroom.

In the lunch room, Simon sits facing Jilla and Almont sits to Jilla's left. They eat quietly until Simon asks, "Jilla, why does your fifth cousin live in the forbidden woods?" Jilla replies, "I don't know. My parents never talk about her. I just know we're very distantly related because of our family tree book." Almont remarks, "That bitter, decrepit crow's your cousin. Good thing looks aren't necessarily inherited hey." Jilla taps Almont on the shoulder. Almont says, "I'm kidding but seriously you should be happy you look nothing like her." Jilla smiles and says, "Okay I'm happy I don't look like her! No one in my family does." Simon finishes chewing and swallowing his muffin. He says, "I read in the sacred doctrine that all Dreamvillians are forbidden to live in the forest wall and she lives in a shack in the forest wall." Almont says, "We read that too. Didn't we Jilla?" Jilla nods her head in agreement. Simon says, "Intriguing. Every time I ask an adult about her, no one gives me a straight answer, she lives in the wall of the forbidden forest, plus, she's collecting obsolete computer chips." Jilla asks, "What do you think it all means?" Almont asks, "Yeah what are you assuming?" Simon replies, "I think it all has something to do with a terrible event that took place in Dreamville ten years ago. I overheard my parents discussing just such a thing and they said it happened ten years ago but they were very vague about the details so I still have no idea what happened. I overheard Miss LossDream tell Principal Toombs to try and remember something that happened to him ten years ago while she walked out of his house and that same night I watched Miss DreamNot snooping around outside of Principal Toombs house and she was spreading around some kind of black powdery substance. What I'm assuming; whatever happened involved Principal Toombs, Miss LossDream and Miss DreamNot. Also, the adults know but are keeping it a secret from all of us kids." Jilla says, "That's a lot to take in, in one sitting Simon." The bell rings for class to resume. All three get up from their seats and walk to class. The principal's office door is still closed as they walk by it. With an angry look on his face, Principal Toombs exits from Miss LossDream's classroom. Simon, Jilla and Almont watch him as he storms down the hallway towards them. He leers at them with his yellow eyes and pointy nose as he passes by. Simon asks, "You still think everything's back to normal Almont?" Almont just looks at Simon indicating that he doesn't think everything's back to normal and all three of them enter into the theatre room.

In the theatre room, Simon walks up onto the stage while Jilla and Almont take their seats in the theatre. Simon sits at the piano. Miss LossDream walks into the theatre room from her desk. The class can see she's been crying but she puts on a happy face and says, "Well class I leave you to Simon's disposal in order to get this show on the road. Simon, work your genius." Miss LossDream takes a seat in the theatre. Simon stands up and says, "I'd like to make a small change to my piece. I want Jilla MusiDream to be the lead female vocal and Brunei Dreamilee as the lead male vocal." Both hear their names and walk up onto the stage to stand by the piano. The rehearsal begins and lasts the whole afternoon. Every element flows fluently into the next without hesitation or interruption. At the end of the day, Miss LossDream says, "That was a great rehearsal. I think we're ready to present this piece and film it as well! Good job everybody and an excellent job Simon!" She and the whole class claps. Simon gets up from the piano and says, "Thank you. I feel I have to say that this piece deeply touches me and for me, it's not about the money but the message this piece conveys. I'll see everyone tomorrow night. Opening night! Sweet Dreams." They all clap their hands and start leaving the theatre room to go home. Miss LossDream walks up to Simon and says, "You're a truly gifted boy Simon Dreamlee. Go home and get a good night's sleep and don't overexert yourself during the day. Sweet dreams!" Miss LossDream exits the theatre room. Almont and Jilla walk up to Simon with their smiles. Jilla enthusiastically says, "Thank you Simon for making me the lead female vocal!" She hugs him and kisses him on his cheek. Suddenly, Rino DreamScifi says, "Jilla, I'm waiting for you hon." Jilla stops hugging Simon and smiles at Almont. She says, "Well I better go. My boyfriend wants to walk me home today. Bye boys and sweet dreams."

Almont says, "Yeah bye. Sweet dreams." Simon who's still blushing says, "See you tomorrow night. Sweet dreams!" They watch Jilla run up the stairs to Rino and they kiss on the lips. Rino holds her hand and Jilla waves goodbye to Simon and Almont. They exit the theatre room. Almont says, "Well at least now Jilla's out of our hair hey." Simon says, "Yeah, girl germs and that type of thing. Hey isn't Rino like three years older than us?" Almont says, "Yeah two years, she'll eventually realize that he's too old for her." Simon smiles and says, "Let's go home my friend. Let's go home." They walk up the theatre steps and exit the theatre room. They walk down the hallway and as they're about to go out the front door they hear a crash. They run in the direction of the noise. It brings them to the gymnasium for the sports inclined dreamers.

Once in the dark gymnasium, they notice the light is still on in the sports coach's office, they walk towards the office and look inside. They see Miss DreamNot with dozens of boxes of obsolete computer chips. Simon says, "She's sneaking them out the side door to her car." Almont and Simon tip-toe out of the gymnasium into the hallway and out the front door to the side of the school where they observe her until she's done transferring all the boxes into her hover car. Almont asks, "What do you think she's doing?" Simon says, "I don't know but whatever it is you can be sure that Principal Toombs is the mastermind behind this charade." Almont looks at his digital watch's computer screen and says, "Well we better get home Simon." Simon nods his head to agree with Almont and they quietly make their way to the hover bike parkade. Simon gets on his hover bike, Almont stands on his hover board and they hover quickly to their intersection of Dreamway Street and ValleysDream Drive. They stop and hover stilly in the air. Simon says, "After tomorrow night, we have to investigate." Almont says, "I agree but for now let's go home and get some sleep. Sweet dreams Simon." Simon says, "Sweet Dreams Almont." They hover their separate ways. Simon hovers into his backyard and parks his hover bike to get recharged with the solar energy collected during the day by the solar panels. He gets off his hover bike and goes inside his house.

Once inside, he walks into the kitchen and sits at the kitchen table. Mrs. Dreamlee walks in and says, "Simon dear, supper is pumpkin pie with dream whip! Yum! Here you go. Oh and don't disturb your father tonight. He's having some important clients over after dinner." Simon says, "Sure, no problem. On that same note, you both will be coming to my opening night tomorrow right?" Simon's mom smiles and says, "Of course dear, we wouldn't miss it for the world." She exits the kitchen.

Simon eats his supper and drinks his chocolate milk from their brown cow, Korteny. He walks upstairs past his parent's room where he waves at his mother who's reading a book while lying on her bed and up the second set of stairs to the attic to unwind with some simple star gazing. Simon says, "This will surely help me to relax." He sets up his microscope and changes the coordinates to look up into the sky at the stars. His pet bird lands on his telescope. Simon says, "There you are. Did you have a nice flight?" His bird chirps at him. Simon laughs and the bird flies downstairs right into its cage. Simon looks through his telescope at the stars as they start to come out. The moon brightly shines and the stars twinkle gloriously during the stillness of the night. Simon breathes in the fresh air and sighs. He says to his dog who's sitting beside him, "Boomboom Booya today has been an awesome day, almost as awesome as yesterday." Simon's dog wags his tail and barks, "Woof, woof." Simon looks out his telescope once again and says, "Constellations, groups of fixed stars, arbitrarily considered together, named because of an imaginary outline enclosing them. How wonderfully relaxing they are!" Out of the blue, his dog knocks over his telescope. Simon says, "Whoa!" he catches it before it falls to the floor and smashes. He places it back on the stand and looks through it to make sure the magnifying glass has not been broken. Simon says, "Looks like everything's fine. Wait what's this?" He observes Miss LossDream leaving Principal Toombs house in tears. Simon says, "What does she see in him? I see nothing but evilness." Principal Toombs walks outside but it's too late Miss LossDream has already hovered away in her hover car. He appears to be crying too. He falls to his knees and puts his head in his hands. He stays that way for a good couple of minutes. When he finally stands up he looks like his usual self again, mean, cruel, conniving and scary. The perplexing quick change in Principal Toombs personality intrigues Simon. Simon says, "I think tomorrow I will pay a visit to his house while he's at school performing his duties as a principal. After all, only the musically inclined dreamers have no school because of my production. There could be a crucial clue in his house." Principal Toombs walks back into his house and slams the door. With that scene over, Simon decides to go to bed without being told. He walks to the second floor. He can faintly here his father with his clients discuss their new technological plans but can't really make out what they're saying. Simon's mom comes out of her room and says, "They're using a voice camouflage that muffles their words so no one can listen in on their secret inventions." Simon looks at his mother and says, "Interesting. Can anyone buy one of those?" She nods her head,

"No dear, it's a secret invention of your great, great grand-father and he wanted his invention to remain a secret for fear it might end up in the wrong hands. So keep this a, shush, between us okay." She winks at him. Simon says, "Okay mom. No problem. I'm going to bed. Sweet dreams!" Mrs. Dreamlee says, "Sweet dreams son!" She closes her bedroom door. Simon goes into his room and closes his door too.

In his bedroom, he sits on his bed petting his dog. Simon says, "Everything, Boomboom Booya, is not back to normal and that's why, first thing tomorrow morning, I'll sneak into Principal Toombs house. I'll bring my virtual camera to take pictures of the clue or clues. It's the perfect day, there's no chance that I'll get caught." Simon walks to his window and looks into the backyard and says, "I'll have to be careful not to leave evidence that I was there. I know what to do. I'll put plastic bags over my shoes to camouflage my shoe prints and I'll wear rubber gloves to prevent my finger prints from getting on stuff I might have to touch." He walks back to his bed, climbs under the covers and attaches his dream catcher to his head. Simon says to his dog, "Sweet Dreams Boomboom Booya." As per Dreamvillians tradition, as soon as his head touches his pillow, he's fast asleep and comfortably dreaming.

He doesn't dream about anything new. Simon dreams about his present dream about to come true tomorrow night. He dreams about his whole composition with the dancers, the stage, the singers, the little boy and the musicians as a whole piece from beginning to end. He sleeps with a smile on his face. When suddenly out of the blackness once the little boy who symbolizes hope exits the stage, a flash of an obsolete computer chip, black dust and the sound of the evil woman cackling interrupts the ending and makes him squirm but not wake up. For the rest of his dream that's all he sees over and over until the next day. All he hears is an annoying, evil cackle over and over.

Aha…

Ha-ha…

Aha…

Ha-ha…

Ha

Chapter Eight – Opening Night

Bright and early at six AM Wednesday morning, Simon wakes up and stretches his arms. He detaches his dream catcher from his head and decides not to review it until after the performance. He gets out of bed and goes downstairs to eat breakfast. His parents are already gone to work. Simon says, "Wow, they must have had to get to work earlier than usual today." He turns on the virtualcast to listen to the news. The clown reporter says, "Another, you guessed it, dreamy day in Dreamville with no clouds in sight. Sunshine will dominate the day from morning until night. How dreamy and speaking of dreamy dreams, Simon Dreamlee's debuting his latest dream tonight at the Dreamtrue Theatre at six PM. To purchase a ticket to his dream come true, please contact our local Dreamville virtual ticket seller for your seat number. Tickets range between one hundred and fifty to five hundred dream dollars. However, I know many of you dreamy Dreamvillians already have your tickets and that's the reason you're all at work earlier than usual today. I wish a happy Wednesday to everyone." Simon turns off the virtualcast and looks in the fridge for breakfast. Simon says, "I have a craving for a piece of blueberry cake." He takes his cake to the attic, eats it as he watches Principal Toombs leave his house, get in his hover car and hover in the direction of the school. Simon says, "Great, now I'll just wait one more hour for everyone to get to school and then no one will be at home and no one will see me go into his house." Simon runs downstairs to his room and puts the virtual camera, his computer chip sized hand held computer, and his virtual communicator in his pocket. He runs downstairs to the main floor and searches through the drawers in the kitchen for plastic bags. Simon says, "Awe, here are some plastic bags. I'll bring four with me. Now, I have to find rubber gloves." He goes in the laundry and looks in the cupboard where the cleaning robots are kept and he sees orange rubber gloves. Simon says, "Perfect. These will do just fine. Alright, the time, seven thirty AM, I have half an hour to wait before leaving on my investigative mission." He quickly runs to the attic to observe Principal Toombs house until eight AM. Simon says, "Okay, there's nothing unusual or out of the ordinary happening so I'm off to find the clue or clues." He runs downstairs to the main floor, through the kitchen, and out into the backyard. He gets on his hover bike and starts hovering towards the hill to Principal Toombs house.

Hovering to the bottom of the hill, Simon looks up, he hadn't factored in the steepness of Principal Toombs hover way driveway. He sits there looking when he gets startled by Almont who hovers up beside him and says, "Simon, are you crazy? What are you doing here?" Simon turns on his hover bike and they both hover in the air. Simon replies, "I think I'll ask the questions. Why are you here? How did you find me?" Almont says, "I was hovering up to your house to ask you to come play virtual video games with me for the day and I saw you hover out of your hover way in this direction so, naturally, I followed you. Are you going to answer my questions now?" Simon looks at him and says, "Alright, I'll tell you. I decided last night after witnessing Miss LossDream leaving Principal Toombs house in tears again…" Almont interrupts, "Wait again? When was this?" Simon replies, "Last night." Almont says, "Last night?" Simon says, "Yes now listen. I decided to sneak into Principal Toombs house to find a clue or clues." Almont says, "What clue or clues?" Simon says, "I don't know yet that's why I have to sneak in his house to find them." Almont says, "Okay, well, I'm not letting you go in there alone." Simon says, "Great, put these plastic bags on your feet so your shoe prints can't be traced and I only have one pair of rubber gloves so make sure you don't touch anything or else they'll be able to trace your finger prints." Almont says, "You're thorough." He takes the plastic bags and puts them on his feet and Simon does the same. Simon puts the rubber gloves on and looks at Almont and he says, "Ready Almont?" Almont gulps and nods his head. They hover up the steep hill to Principal Toombs house. They hover to his doorstep and park their hover bikes by the steps out of sight. Simon walks up the steps with Almont following right behind him. Almont says, "This place is creepy. I can't believe you dared and did come here at night." Simon hushes him, "Shush." Simon looks inside for a security system but sees none. Simon says, "No security system so I can pick the lock the old fashioned way with one of my mother's hair pins." Simon checks his pockets and miraculously has one in his pocket. Simon says, "I have no idea why I have a hair pin in my pocket but it's a good thing I do." He sticks the pin in the old lock and hears it click. He turns and looks at Almont as he turns the knob and opens the door. They walk inside the decrepit, run down, ill maintained house.

Once inside, they look around the giant room of the main floor. Almont say, "There are no walls at all. This place is huge." Simon says, "It's so dark in here too and look there's the smashed dream catcher. He hasn't cleaned it up or fixed it." Almont says, "There's nothing to see here Simon. He has centuries' old, tattered furniture and look in his cupboard, all his dishes are cracked and stained by rusty water." Simon looks through the drawers and finds nothing and he says, "Drawers and drawers of tarnished utensils that in their glory must have been bright silver." Almont says, "It seems like this place should be intimidating us with its richness but it's not." Simon looks at the numerous huge dusty, blackened crystal chandeliers and light fixtures and says, "I know what you're saying. Well we'll go upstairs and search up there." They both go upstairs and find nothing but a bed with semi new sheets and a bathroom with rusted faucets. He doesn't have a dresser or a closet with clothes. Almont says, "I guess we know why he always wears the same clothes every day." Simon looks in the other three large bedrooms and there's nothing in them, not even furniture. Almont says, "Okay Simon I'm beginning to think that we're not going to find anything here to incriminate Principal Toombs in any kind of evil plot." Simon sighs and says, "You might be right. I guess it's back downstairs." They go downstairs to the main floor and as Almont opens the door to leave, Simon says, "Almont here's the basement door" Almont says, "This creepy place has a basement? Are you going to go down there?" Simon goes down the stairs and Almont rolls his eyes and follows Simon down the stairs to another wide open, dark, dank and musty space. Almont says, "You know this place would be grand if only he had a personality transplant." Simon says, "Okay we better get out of here." They run up the unstable stairs and out of the house. Simon shuts the door behind them and makes sure it's locked. They walk to their hover bikes by the steps. Simon pulls out his computer chip sized computer and tries to log onto the internet. Simon says, "Log on the internet. I can't get on the internet. It's like something's scrambling my signal." Almont pulls his out of his pocket and tries logging onto the internet too. Almont says, "Log on the internet. That's odd I can't access the internet either. Why do you need the internet now anyway?" Simon says, "That's not important right now. What's important is figuring out what is scrambling our signals." Simon looks at the ground at the withered, dead remnants of plants and looks at the soil. Almont asks, "What are you looking at?" Simon gets on his hover bike and so does Almont. Simon hovers closely to the ground, takes off one of the plastic bags and has his hover bike's hand claw scoop up a sample of the dirt. Simon says, "Okay, I got the clue we were looking for now we'll get out of here before we get caught." Simon quickly hovers down the hill with Almont close behind him. They hover all the way to Simon's house and park in his back yard.

Simon and Almont get off of their hover bikes and go inside the house. Almont asks, "Are you going to tell me why you collected dirt from Principal Toombs yard?" Simon puts the tightly closed bag of dirt on the kitchen table. He pulls out his computer chip sized computer and tries to access the internet. Simon says, "Log on the internet. Look at that. I can access the internet now. Almont quick try yours." Almont pulls out his hand held computer and it works fine too. Almont says, "Log on the internet. Well I'm shocked. I remember you mentioning seeing Miss DreamNot spreading a black powdery substance around Principal Toombs yard…" Simon interrupts Almont, "Exactly, this dirt has some of that black powder in it and I'm going to get it tested." Simon looks at the bag and takes off the other bag and puts it in the garbage. He gets a newer bag from the drawer and double bags the dirt. Almont takes the bags on his feet off and puts them in the garbage too. Almont asks, "Simon who are you going to get to test this dirt? I mean, you'll have to tell them where you got it from and then they'll know that we sneaked around his yard and house." Simon says, "Jilla's boyfriend. I'll talk to Jilla and she'll convince him to do the testing and not tell on us. What we're doing here, today, this very moment, is for the greater good and may actually help Principal Toombs. Almont, I'm positive this substance, mixed with Dreamville's soil, is causing him some form of harm." Simon and Almont go up to the attic and Simon hides the dirt in a metal box. Simon says, "For now, the dirt should be safe here." Almont says, "Look at the time. Four PM, I better get back home, wash and get ready for opening night. You better get your mind off of this and get ready too." Simon says, "I'll see you at the theatre." They give each other a high five, Almont quickly goes downstairs and out the back door to his hover bike and hovers towards his house. Simon goes to the bathroom, shuts the door and takes a half hour shower.

Half an hour later, Simon's ready to make his way to Dreamtrue School and début his controversial dream. He walks downstairs and his mother's waiting for him in the kitchen. She says, "Are you ready to go?" Simon smiles at her and says, "This is it! I'm ready!" She smiles at him and they walk out of the house and get in the hover car. Hovering to the

Dreamtrue Theatre, Mrs. Dreamlee says, "I'm proud of you son! Have fun tonight and remember do not talk to the media clowns." Simon nods his head in agreement. She pulls into the hover car parkade and they go in the side door of the theatre and Simon joins the rest of the cast. They wait silently backstage for the clock to indicate six PM. They listen to the crowd quietly chattering as they enter the theatre and sit in their seats. Miss LossDream puts her hand on Simon's shoulder as he peers through the curtain at the gathering crowd and she says, "Knock them dead tonight Simon! Ha-ha. That's another theatre saying. Best of luck and you'll do well." Simon says, "Thank you Miss LossDream." She goes around to the front and sits in the audience by Principal Toombs. Simon can see that everybody in Dreamville's attending his production. He can also see the hover film crew setting up to turn this production into a movie for the outsiders. Simon sees his father walk in the theatre, he kisses his mother on the lips and they sit in their seats. He looks at the time as the lights dim in the theatre. Simon turns around and softly says to the cast who are already in the opening positions, "This is it! Good luck everyone!" Simon walks to the side of the stage to the white grand piano and sits on the bench. Adorning the piano are four antique gold candle holders with tall white candles. Jilla looks angelic dressed in a gold dress to match the set. Brunei's black tuxedo compliments Simon's more modern black suit. The set darkens as the ballet begins in darkness. They all wait for the curtain to open.

The curtain opens and Simon begins to softly play along with the other musicians he picked to accompany him. The audience already begins to clap but quickly quiets down as the two lovers dance on the stage. The silvery stage glimmers like stars and moonlight and is surrounded by fresh wild flowers. The scent of the wild flowers fills the theatre. The members of the audience are entranced by the lyrical music all about the love between the true lovers. They're drawn into the story being portrayed on the stage by the graceful movements and facial expressions of the dancers. The singers sing the lyrics elegantly, slowly and sophisticatedly with believable emotion. The emotion of the dancers and the singers infects the audience as they connect with the love story. The lights shining on the dancers, immediately the audience understands the symbolism and easily they can imagine the lights are really coming from within the two lovers. The music increases, the drum beat symbolizing the heart beats gets louder, the lovers love glows more and more brightly. The glow, lights the theatre as the two embrace and kiss on the stage. The audience claps until the sudden change in the music, the dramatic violin begins, the drum beats continues and the evil third woman enters the scene. The audience gasps while being drawn further into the dramatic end to true love as the evil woman wraps the black material around the man. The black material symbolizes the woman's plot succeeding and the destruction of the man's love for his true love. The stage darkens with only the flicker of the candles from Simon's piano as he plays with the violinist. The second female dancer takes her position on the stage as on onlooker and cackles. The continuous drum beat beats rhythmically as the man's true love enters on the stage, her light lights up the scene. Just like in Simon's dream, she happily dances up to her lover who performs jerky dance movements symbolizing his inner turmoil. She dances up to him to kiss him and he turns away. She holds her heart and dances her way to the side of the stage and pulls out the ceramic red heart, drops it on the stage and as it shatters, the drum beat stops. The symbolism that her heart is broken is clearly conveyed to the audience as many start to cry. The only instrument playing is the violin. The sound from the violin is painfully eerie yet filled with profoundly deep agonizing sorrow. The scene pulls at the heart strings of the audience. The man alone on the stage holds his head in his hands and symbolically dances around the stage portraying the man's struggle with the loss of his true love. Already dim, his light goes completely out as darkness surrounds him. Stopping in the middle of the stage, the man takes his hand onto his heart and pulls the black dust out and drops it on the stage. The woman who was once the object of his affection watches him on the side with her light shining brightly cries in agony, with movements and facial expression displaying her broken heart and pain she exits the stage. The evil woman plays her part and dances up to the man a dim red light shines down on them and he pushes her away from him when she tries to kiss him. Their dance movements symbolize a fight, a struggle and the message that he rejects this evil woman's advances. He holds his heart and with desperation on his face he exits the stage with large dance strides. The evil woman alone on the stage cackles. The light goes out on the stage. The violins music ends dramatically. No sound fills the theatre except the crying audience members. Simon timed his piece this way for effect. The little boy appears on the stage as the bright light shines down the key on his neck. Simon begins to play the piano and this time just the piano as the angelic smooth voices of the lead singers fill the theatre with hope. The boy dancer dances with small innocent movements and ends looking out into the audience at the same moment the fluttery music stops. The light remains shining on him for an extra minute longer, then the stage goes dark. The curtains close and the cast gathers behind the curtain for when the curtain opens again so they can take a bow. The audience erupts in cheers, clapping and whistling. "Bravo, bravo, bravo. Encore, Encore. Bravo!" The audience stands on their feet expression their appreciation for this new form of artistic expression and the cast takes a bow. Simon looks out into the audience and sees Principal Toombs is hiding his tears while he quickly wipes his face with a dirty handkerchief. The audience yells, "Spectacular, bravo!" Miss LossDream walks on the stage and gives the female cast members long stemmed red roses and shakes the hands of the male cast members. The curtain closes and the production is a success. The audience begins their chatter as they try and make their way out of the theatre but before anyone leaves, the entire theatre goes black, everyone gasps and hushes quickly as a mysterious woman's voice says "They're never going to get their true love back. Ha-ha. Ha-ha, Ha-ha." The lights come back on and everyone starts chattering while they leave the theatre in shock. Miss LossDream grabs Simon's arm and angrily asks, "What was that? That wasn't a part of the plans?" Simon replies, "I don't know what that was. I didn't plan that at all. You can ask anyone of the cast members." Almont says, "It's true. We were all taken by surprise when that happened." Miss LossDream says, "Alright then, I guess it's just someone doing some kind of practical joke. Go home boys. Go home everyone. Oh yes and Bravo" She blows a kiss to the cast members. Jilla says, "Sweet dreams everyone." She goes to meet Rino and both of their parents.

Simon and Almont find their parents having a conversation with each other. Mr. Dreamlee says, "Well son, that was amazing. You're a good producer in my mind and Mayor Alldream agrees." Mayor Alldream says, "Definitely a great production!" Simon says, "Thanks sir." Mayor Alldream says, "Well my son, we should be getting home. Sweet Dreams everyone." Almont says, "Sweet dreams." Mr. and Mrs. Dreamlee say, "Sweet dreams." Simon says, "See you tomorrow. Sweet dreams." Looking around the Dreamlee's notice they're the only ones left in the theatre. Successfully avoiding the media clowns, they walk out of the side door to the theatre to their hover car, get in and start hovering for home. Mr. Dreamlee asks, "What happened at the end there, son?" Simon shakes his head and says, "I have no idea. Miss LossDream thinks someone was trying to pull off a practical joke." Mrs. Dreamlee says, "Well thank goodness it didn't ruin the night." Mr. Dreamlee says, "That's right, it almost seemed to fit in with your production." Simon smiles and says, "In a way but certainly not something I would have done. None the less my dream came true tonight. I'm happy!" Mrs. Dreamlee says, "Good Simon, very good." Mr. Dreamlee turns into the hover driveway and into their garage. Visibly tired, yawning, they get out and go in their house.

Once inside, they're shocked out of their sleepiness when they discover the house has been ransacked for a second time. This time the house has been completely turned upside down with the furniture knocked down everywhere. Mrs. Dreamlee screams, "Who would do this?" Mr. Dreamlee remains calm and says, "I don't know dear. Everyone was at the theatre tonight. The whole population of Dreamville was there. I better get the dream squad on virtual wave and have them come and look at the crime scene." Simon quickly runs upstairs to the attic and looks in the metal tin box. He finds the plastic bag filled with dirt from Principal Toombs yard has been stolen. Simon says, "Why would someone steal a bag of dirt unless they know that I might discover something bad. I'm right that black powder must be tested." Simon ran back downstairs and says, "I know who did this, I know." Mr. Dreamlee's on the virtual wave talking to the Dream squad chief and they say, "Who Simon? Miss DreamNot did this." The dream squad chief says, "Son that's a guess and only a guess. I'm sure she's not involved in this in any way. Now Mr. Dreamlee we'll be right over to investigate and gather evidence. Bye" Mr. Dreamlee says, "Bye." Simon runs to the drawer with plastic bags and then he runs out to his bike. He hovers off in the direction of Principal Toombs house. He sees that he's home so he quietly hovers at the edge of his yard and uses the mechanical hand from his hover bike to reach into his yard and fill the plastic bags with the blackened powdery dirt. He quickly seals the bag tightly as Principal Toombs opens his door and screams, "Who's there? You dare to try and rob me while I'm home? I'll catch you." Simon quickly hovers down the hill and takes back alleys back to his home. He makes it home to see the dream squad leaving. He pulls into the backyard and parks his hover bike. He quickly goes in the already cleaned up house, past the cleaning robots and runs up to the attic. He puts the bags of dirt in the metal tin container and carries it to his already cleaned up room. He hides it under his bed. He hears his mother coming up the stairs, she pokes her head in his room and says, "Simon dear, where were you? The dream squad investigators wanted to talk to you about your accusations against Miss DreamNot? I'll let you know they don't think it was her." Simon says, "How can they not think it was her? Personally, I didn't see her at my production." Mrs. Dreamlee says, "Oh about that. The film producers called and they need to discuss the contract with you. It seems they want to increase your pay and they want the rights to be the ones who film the sequel. You have a meeting tomorrow morning and then you'll go to school in the afternoon." Simon says, "That's great mom. What about Miss DreamNot?" Mrs. Dreamlee says, "I think that, that's your overactive imagination son. Love you but it's time for bed. Sweet dreams." She shuts his bedroom door.

Simon sits on the chair at his desk in his room. He looks out the window and sees the Dream squad at another house and yet another. Simon says, "Those adults including my own parents are still hiding something. I'm going to discover Dreamville's secret past." He observes the dream investigators leaving people's houses with dismay, shock and complete and utter cluelessness written all over their faces. Simon says, "They're dumbfounded. If only they would listen to me. I have proof but I can't tell them she stole my bag of dirt or else they'll know I've been snooping around at Principal Toombs house." Suddenly, his virtual communicator sounds off and Almont appears on the virtual wave saying, "Simon, hey Simon are you awake?" Simon says, "Almont I'm awake. What is it?" Almont says, "We were robbed while we were at the theatre." Simon says, "So were we along with three other family's houses on my street and I know who did it." Almont says, "Who? It can't be Principal Toombs because he was at the production from the beginning to the end." Simon says, "Yes he was and he was hiding his tears." Almont says, "He was?" Simon says, "Yeah but that's not important right now. I think Miss DreamNot robs Dreamvillians and rummages through the garbage bins at night too because she wasn't at the theatre tonight. Everything leads up to her being up to something." Almont says, "Well I believe your hunch after seeing her with all those boxes of obsolete computer chips." Simon says, "Almont I have a meeting about my contract tomorrow morning and then I'll meet you at school in the afternoon. After school we have to talk to Jilla and her boyfriend Rino. Rino, being a science inclined dreamer will surely have the skills to test the dirt. Oh yeah and that's the other reason Miss DreamNot is my prime suspect. The original bag of dirt was stolen and I had to sneak out and go get another two samples. I almost got caught tonight." Almont says, "Okay I'll see you tomorrow afternoon. I have to go I hear my parents coming upstairs. Sweet Dreams." The virtual communicator shuts off and Simon climbs into his bed. He attaches the dream catcher to his head and puts his head on the pillow. He instantly falls to sleep.

With his production done and complete, he's free to dream about new unrelated compositions but he doesn't. He dreams about the production in its entirety with the added additional blackness at the end and the flash vision of a single computer chip. For the first time ever, Simon tosses and turns all night long. He's so disruptive while he sleeps that he accidentally kicks his Boomboom Booya off of his bed. Boomboom Booya goes to sleep on the floor, in a corner in Simon's room. The evil woman's cackles and cackles until he wakes up the next morning. For the second night in a row, Simon's dream is filled with the evil woman's laughter.

Ha-ha,
Ha-ha,
Aha.

Chapter Nine – Dreamvillians Are Stunned

Thursday morning, Simon wakes up to the chatter of his parents in their bedroom. He also sees that his bedroom door is already open. He detaches the dream catcher from his head and he tip toes to his parent's doorway and listens. Mrs. Dreamlee says, "What do you mean you didn't have a dream?" Mr. Dreamlee replies, "I mean I didn't dream up any new invention or even about old ones. I did not dream. It's like I shut my eyes when it was dark out and opened them now that it's light outside." He puts his head in his hands. Mrs. Dreamlee says, "No, this can't be happening. Honey this is what happened to him before…" Mr. Dreamlee interrupts and says, "I know. I don't want you to worry. I'll go to work today and my fellow colleagues and I will figure out what causes this phenomenon." Mrs. Dreamlee says, "Oh please do, I don't want to lose you. Simon and I don't want to lose you." Simon tip toes downstairs and into the kitchen. Simon whispers, "What's happening?" His mother walks in the kitchen with her happy face and says, "Well Simon, are you ready to go and negotiate your new contract? Come now, it's time to go!" Simon says, "Sure mom. Mom is there anything wrong?" She smiles at him and says, "No, of course not dear. Come on!" They walk out of the house and into the garage. They get in the hover car and hover to Dreamville Films and Movies Production Company on Dreamwood Boulevard. Mrs. Dreamlee turns into the hover car parkade and says, "Wow look at this place. It's so dreamy!" Simon says, "It really is dreamy. Well time to go inside and make money." They get out of the car and walk into the lobby of the gigantic building. Mrs. Dreamlee walks up to the administrative assistant and says, "Happy Thursday. Simon Dreamlee's here for his early appointment." The administrative assistant says, "Great, please have a seat over here in the dream lounge area and I'll call you when Mr. MakesFilmDreams is ready to see him." They silently sit in the lounge for over an hour. The time seemingly goes by quickly as virtual posters of past, current and future movies pop up periodically to advertise the story premises and viewing times in the Dreamville Movie Theatre. Finally, the administrative assistant says, "Mr. MakesFilmDreams is available to see you now Mr. Dreamlee." Simon stands up and looks at his mom. She smiles, winks and says, "Go on. You can do this without me." Simon smiles and walks across the long floor and he enters into the movie producer's office.

Simon walks into the giant white room, with white furniture adorned in gold accents everywhere. Mr. MakesFilmDreams says with his boisterous and booming voice, "Come in, Simon Dreamlee. We have much to discuss this morning. Here, sit over here." Simon walks across the room and sits in the giant plush gold velvet chair and waits for the producer to start the negotiations. Simon smiles at Mr. MakesFilmDreams while he smiles back at him. The producer breaks the silence and says, "Simon Dreamlee, you're a talented twelve year old boy aren't you. This last production of yours is the buzz in the entertainment industry. The show you put on last night was an absolute hit with everyone in Dreamville. Now, here is the contract I want to offer you. You will get an initial payment of five million dollars. Your cast will be paid three point five million each. With the export of your dream come true to the outsiders, you will be paid a substantial amount of royalties as it makes money in movie theatres. My offer is for each ten dollars the movie version of your dream come true makes, you'll earn two dollars and your cast members will make one dollar. We also want to pay you initially six million dollars to assure we are the ones who produce the sequel. What do you think?" Simon says, "That sounds great but I want to take a few moments to think about it before I sign." The producer says, "Go ahead Simon and read it. I'm confident you'll be satisfied with the wording of this document." Mr. MakesFilmDreams steps out of his office for twenty minutes while Simon reads the contract.

Twenty minutes later, Mr. MakesFilmDreams walks back into his office and says, "Well dear boy, what have you decided?" He walks around to his desk and sits in his seat to wait for Simon's answer. Simon stands up and extends his hand and says, "I like this contract." Mr. MakesFilmDreams takes Simons hand, shakes it and says, "That's great Simon. Here is my pen and you can sign on the dotted line right here." Simon releases his grip and takes the pen. He signs the contract and they both smile at each other. Mr. MakesFilmDreams says, "I'm looking forward to working with you some more in the near future. Simon smiles and says, "As am I with you Mr. MakesFilmDreams. Well I must be going now. I have school this afternoon. Good Thursday!" The producer replies, "Absolutely, good

Thursday, oh and here is your copy of the agreement. Don't lose this now." Simon smiles, takes his copy of the contract and walks out of his office. Mrs. Dreamlee walks up to him with a smile and they leave the building. She says, "I see things worked out well." Simon says, "Very well mother. I'm quite happy with the contract and I think my cast will be too." They get to the hover car and climb inside. Simon's mom says, "Looks like you'll get to school just on time for lunch." They hover to Dreamtrue School. Simon gets out of the Hover car and says, "Happy Thursday mom, I'll see you tonight." She waves at him as he walks into the front door of the school.

Once in the hallway of the school, Simon walks to the lunchroom past Principal Toombs office. The office door is shut again. He walks into the lunchroom and waits the five minutes for the lunch bell to ring. Principal Toombs walks into the lunchroom and says, "Well, well, look who decided to show up at school today." Simon says, "I had a contract meeting this morning." Principal Toombs says, "Of course you did." Simons says, "Well I guess you can't be happy for me right now." Principal Toombs says, "I will never be happy for you and any of your fellow student's dreams coming true. I still say life is not a dream." Simon says, "I don't believe you truly think that way Principal Toombs. I saw you hide your tears at my production last night." Principal Toombs lunges at Simon, leans over him in an intimidating way and screams, "You saw no such thing Simon Dreamlee. You're not only a trouble maker but a fabricator of lies." The lunch bell rings and the students enter into the lunch room. Principal Toombs slinks out of the room leaving Simon visibly shaken and alone at his table. Rino asks, "What was he telling you?" Simon says, "Nothing useful. Don't worry about it." Rino acknowledges Simons right to privacy and sits with the science inclined dreamers. Now, the musically inclined dreamers start entering the lunch room and Almont sits with Simon. Simon asks, "Good Thursday?" Almont says, "Not really. We just had a terrible class this morning. Twelve of our colleagues didn't have a dream to view this morning. They all claim they didn't dream last night." Simon says, "What? Twelve people didn't dream." Almont says, "Yeah, they described it as being like they closed their eyes when it was dark and opened them when it was light. Can you imagine not dreaming? I'd go ballistic." Simon says, "Look there's Jilla sitting with Rino." Almont looks and says, "Uh... they're always smooching on the lips." Simon says, "Almont we have to get her to talk to him about testing the soil samples." Almont asks, "How do you propose we do that without arousing their suspicions." Simon says, "Lately, they're always walking home from school together. We'll catch them after school and talk to them privately." The bell rings to indicate the start of the afternoon classes. Simon and Almont walk back to class past Principal Toombs office, the door's open and they see Miss DreamNot glaring at them as they walk by. Almont says, "Creepy. She sends cold shivers up and down my spine." Simon says, "I know exactly what you mean."

Once in their seats in their musically inclined classroom, Miss LossDream walks in and sits at her desk like she usually does. Miss LossDream gets up and the class hushes. She says, "Simon Dreamlee, I'm happy to see you've come to class this afternoon. I'd be out celebrating if I were you. I was watching the virtualcast during lunch break and it seems Simon you have signed a rather lucrative movie deal for your dream come true and the sequel. Congratulations!" The class claps their hands and cheers. Simon says, "Thank you. All the cast members will be very well paid as well so of course that means all of you." They all clap some more until Miss LossDream signals to hush. Miss LossDream continues to say, "It also seems that apart from the multiple break and enters that occurred last night during Simon's dream come true production that there's another more serious epidemic occurring in Dreamville. I acted harshly and for that I'm sorry to the twelve of you. On the virtualcast they announced a serious problem being reported by countless members of Dreamville. It seems people's dreams are being stolen from them while they sleep. Many of you complained about not dreaming last night and I didn't believe you but I believe you now. The class is dismissed for the rest of the afternoon until tomorrow. You may all go home." The students get out of their seats and start leaving the classroom. Once Simon and Almont are in the corridor, they can see that the whole school has been told to go home. Simon says, "Quickly we have to find Jilla and Rino." Almont squints and says, "Not hard to do, just follow the smooching sounds." Jilla and Rino are smooching while standing outside in front of the school on the sidewalk. Simon and Almont go outside and interrupt their smooching time. Simon says, "Jilla, Rino there's plenty of time for that later. Can I have a moment of both of your time?" Jilla is visibly annoyed with the interruption but Rino answers first, "Sure Simon." Simon looks around and says, "Not here. We need to find some place more private." Rino says, "There's nowhere more private than my personal laboratory at my house." Almont says, "That's perfect." Simon says, "Indeed, we just have to stop at my house first. I have to pick something up." Rino says, "Okay, Jilla and I will meet you there. Come with what you have to pick up." Jilla and Rino start to smooch again as they walk towards his house on Dreampond Bay. Almont says, "She's too young to be smooching, especially with a guy as old as him." Simon says, "You're just jealous. Come on. We have to get our hover bikes." Almont shrugs his shoulders, rolls his eyes and says, "I'm not jealous. Why would I be jealous?" They run into the parkade for their hover bikes and get on their hover bikes. They quickly hover to Simon's house and he runs inside to get the metal tin canister with the two soil samples. He runs back outside and gets on his hover bike. They hover to Rino's house as inconspicuously as possible so they don't draw attention to themselves. Almont says, "I was watching the virtualcast while you were getting you know what. The dream squad's everywhere trying to catch the thief they've labeled the dream stealer." Simon says, "We're here, this is his house." They park their hover cars and knock on the door. Rino opens the door and says, "Come in, make yourselves comfortable." Simon gripping his tin canister and Almont wearing a smile on his face walk into Rino's house.

Once inside Rino's house, Simon holds out his tin can for Rino and Jilla to see. Jilla asks, "What's inside your tin canister?" Simon looks around and asks, "Are we alone?" Rino says, "Yeah, my parents are not home before ten PM. They left me a virtual message and they've been called to a secret science meeting by your dad." Simon says, "Good Rino I need you to test these two samples to find out if it's toxic." Rino says, "There's no such soil in Dreamville." Almont says, "This soil's different. The other day Simon and my internet stopped working and our hand held computers were inaccessible when we stood on this soil." Simon explains, "There's weird black dust mixed into this soil and I have come to the conclusion that this black dust is toxic." Rino takes the tin canister from Simon and says, "Well let's see the effects here in my lab. I'll use my hand held computer and see what happens. Come, this way." Jilla, Almont and Simon follow Rino through a long corridor, through the hover car garage into a science room with all kinds of unpatented, un-marketed technological gadgets. Rino puts the tin on the solid wood laboratory table and opens it. He pulls out both bags of soil. He takes a tray from under his table and pours the dirt from one bag into the tray. He looks at Simon and says, "Okay, here it goes." Rino pulls out his computer sized hand held computer and holds it over the soil while he tries to log onto the internet. He pauses, fiddles with the hand held computer and says, "Log on the internet. You're right, I can't get a signal. This soil is contaminated with something that's scrambling my computer's system too." Simon says, "I knew it." Almont says, "This is so unbelievable but I have to believe it because this is all unfolding right in front of my eyes." Simon asks, "Rino how long will it take you to find out with conviction what is the substance in this soil that's causing our hand held computers to be scrambled?" Rino is still observing in awe the effect of the soil on his hand held computer and says, "I can't give you a time frame right now because I need to first decide where to begin testing. It'll be trial and error before I found out the answer. I'm sorry I can't be any more specific than this but that's science." Jilla asks, "Where did you guys find this soil?" Almont says, "Ah… We can't reveal our source just yet." Simon says, "Rino you will do the testing?" Rino says, "I can't resist. My scientific mind has been intrigued and worse boggled." Simon says, "Great Rino, that's absolutely great! You have to promise me to keep this soil hidden from everyone, including your parents." Rino pulls his hand held computer chip sized computer away from the soil and watches how it suddenly starts to work properly. He says, "No problem Simon. I'm going to start working on this right now. I'll contact you as soon as I have results." Almont says, "We better start getting home Simon." Jilla says, "Oh yeah I better leave too Rino." Rino and Jilla kiss and Jilla leaves for her home. Rino says, "This dirt is even more intriguing than the dream stealer and the mysteriously disappearing obsolete computer chips." Simon says, "What, how do you know about the disappearing computer chips?" Rino asks, "How do you know?" Almont says, "We saw Miss DreamNot stealing dozens of boxes of obsolete computer chips from the school a couple days ago." Rino says, "Really, well the technological recycling centre was broken into yesterday and all the stored obsolete computer chips were stolen. They were stored to be recycled but now they're all gone." Simon says, "Why would she want obsolete computer chips?" Rino says, "While you try and figure that out I'll dissect this soil." Simon says, "Good idea! Bye for now Rino." Rino says, "Bye for now." Almont says, "Bye." Simon and Almont leave Rino's house and hover to Simon's house.

Once at Simon's house, Simon runs to his room and looks in his wood chest, hidden way in the back of his closet and opens it. He says, "Look Almont, my obsolete computer chip. That's what she's going around stealing from people. She needs them for something but what." Almont says, "Do you think she has somehow managed to steal people's dreams by possessing our old computer chips?" Simon says, "I'm not sure. She would have had to invent some kind of machine to do that. Where's the machine? It's certainly not in her shack." Almont says, "It's certainly not at Principal Toombs house either." Simon says, "We can't rule out Principal Toombs involvement either. We need to start surveillance of everything those two do every day until we know and then we can present our evidence to the dream squad chief and investigators." Almont says, "Well I better be getting home. My parents will be there soon. Bye for now Simon." Simon says, "Bye for now." Almont runs downstairs and outside to his hover bike, gets on and starts hovering. Simon watches him hover towards his house via the back alley. To prevent his old obsolete computer chip from being stolen, Simon decides to keep his obsolete computer in his pocket. Hungry, he goes downstairs into the kitchen.

Once in the kitchen, he takes out a chocolate cake and has supper while he listens to the virtualcast news program. The clown reporter says, "Dreamvillians are experiencing an unprecedented, unexplainable and unfathomable plague. This plague has affected numerous citizens. Symptoms of the plague are; not dreaming, closing one's eyes when it's dark out and then just opening them when it's light out and involuntary withdrawal from happiness. Other not so dreamy news, there have been numerous reports of break and enters reported by the dreamy citizens of Dreamville. The Dream squad assures us they are working night and day on these two cases. Also, they assure us that there's no possible connection between these two acts of thievery. It has been leaked that the Dreamville Dream science team have been in multiple secret meetings all day to try and solve these mysteries. Don't give up Dreamvillians dreams will still come true." Simon shuts the virtualcast off and puts the remaining chocolate cake back in the fridge. He goes outside and milks Wendy with the hovering milking machine that automatically pasteurizes and chills the milk. He has a fresh glass of cow's milk. Simon says, "Yum, that's good milk." He goes back in his house and goes up to the attic.

Once in the attic, he looks out through his telescope. Simon whispers to himself, "I'll observe all over Dreamville. There's the Dream squad patrolling the streets and back lanes with hover patrol cars. Although this is not typically what's observed in Dreamville, I don't see anything out of the ordinary. I'm going to focus on Principal Toombs house once again." He peers through his telescope up the hill at Principal Toombs House. He sees a Dream squad car leaving his yard and Principal Toombs enters his house and slams the door. Simon focuses back on the street and sees his parents hover car coming towards the house. They pull into the garage and Simon hears his father calling him, "Simon, son, are you home?" Simon runs down the two sets of stairs to welcome his parents' home. He says, "I'm here." He runs into the kitchen. His father is standing in the kitchen, facing the window, eating a piece of chocolate cake. He asks, "So son, I hear you're happy with your contract." Simon says, "Yeah I am. It's a great contract." He turns around and Simon sees his father's eyes are not quite yellow but they're yellowing just like Principal Toombs. Simon's eyes grow big and he asks, "Dad, are you feeling okay?" Simon's dad says, "Oh yeah, I think I may be developing some kind of allergy. It's nothing for you to worry about. Well son, time for you to go to bed. Sweet Dreams." Simon says, "Sweet dreams dad." He starts walking out of the kitchen and turns around and says, "Don't worry dad, I'm working on solving this whole situation." Simon runs upstairs and into his bedroom. He shuts his door and decides to enter all his clues in his hand held computer. He makes sure his bedroom windows are closed. As he voice records them into his personalized computer, he realizes that all his computer chips may get scrambled within the next couple of hours. He writes the clues on a piece of paper while he voice records them, "First clue, Miss LossDream argues with Principal Toombs at his house. Second clue, the same night, Miss DreamNot was sneaking around outside of Principal Toombs house and she spread around a weird black dust. Third clue, Miss LossDream asks Principal Toombs to remember an event from ten years ago. Note; I also overheard my parents discussing something that happened ten years ago, plus the Dreams quad chief mentioned a crime that happened ten years ago. Fourth clue, Miss DreamNot is a Dreamvillian who lives in a shack in the forbidden wall of the forest. Fifth clue, Almont and I saw her stealing dozens of boxes of computer chips. Sixth clue, a robbing spree and only obsolete computer chips are stolen. Seventh clue, the original soil sample I collected from Principal Toombs yard was stolen. Eighth clue, this soil scrambles and stops our computers signals. Ninth clue, today, overheard my father say his dream was stolen and many Dreamvillians have made the exact same claim. Tenth clue, my father's eyes are turning yellow like Principal Toombs and Miss DreamNot's eyes. Eleventh clue, I think my dream come true is linked to what's currently happening." Simon sits on his bed, attaches the dream catcher to his head. He gets up locks his door and climbs into bed. He wants to go to sleep to dream and find out if he'll dream about the sequel. As soon as his head touches the pillow, he starts to sleep.

While sleeping, his dream is filled with darkness and the violin plays a tune that signifies the pain of the many dancers who suddenly appear on the same stage. They have all been wrapped in the same black cloth as the man. They're all holding their heads, their dance movements and facial expressions reflect their agony. The man dances into the centre of the stage while the other dancers dance around him and stop. While stopped they ask what has happened to them but the man indicates he doesn't know. The evil woman dances around the group cackling and she has obsolete computer chips on a rope around her neck. The group dance with fear and submission in their movements and facial expressions. The dream fades to fluttery music. The music plays as a light fills the stage and the little boy with the key around his neck dances freely and happily on the same stage. The boy sings.

Laugh evil,

Laugh evil,

Witch,

I know,

You're just a woman,

Scorned,

Laugh evil,

Laugh evil,

Woman,

I will free everyone,

From you,

And

You will be free from,

You...

Despite the mostly dark overtone of Simon's dream, he sleeps soundly in his room while his dog sleeps at his feet.

Chapter Ten – Chaos in Dreamville

The next morning, Friday morning, the birds chirp, the sun shines, Simon's dog, Boomboom Booya, barks, his cat, Frankie Noodles, scratches at his bedroom door to be let in, but this isn't what wakes Simon from his deep sleep and fascinating dream. "Ahhhhhh... Ah... Ah.... Ahhhhh..." Surprised out of his sleep, Simon wakes up to hear multiple sounds of people screaming. He quickly detaches his dream catcher from his head, puts his computer chip sized hand held computer in his pocket, runs to his bedroom door, unlocks it and runs up to the attic. He looks outside and observes the adults on their knees screaming at the end of their driveways with their heads in their hands. He hears his father's footsteps running downstairs, out the front door to the end of their driveway, he stands and listens to his fellow neighbors screams. Simon looks in his telescope and observes Principal Toombs getting into his hover car and hovers down the steep hill towards his house. Principal Toombs hovers by the screaming citizens and says, "Life's not a dream come true. Now you all will know how I feel. None of you can misunderstand me now. Ha-ha. Aha." Mr. Dreamlee asks, "What have you done Toombs?" Principal Toombs glares at him with his yellow eyes and says, "Nothing. I have done absolutely nothing. This is just a natural phenomenon. Isn't that what you all told me ten years ago? It's the end of Dreamvillians dreams. Ha-ha. Aha." He hovers around and into the direction of Dreamtrue School. Simon sits on the big metal chest in the attic and contemplates Principal Toombs words. He says, "Principal Toombs hasn't dreamed in ten years. That explains his anger and unwillingness to show sadness. Why? Why does he not dream and now suddenly many adults and twelve of his classmates don't dream?" Simon runs out of the attic to his room and grabs his virtual communicator, puts it in his pocket and runs out to his hover bike and starts hovering for Dreamtrue School.

Along the way, Simon sees abandoned hover cars, abandoned hover trucks, abandoned work machines, hovering street lights are flashing and everywhere people are either running or walking at very slow paces. Trees, plants, flowers are beginning to whither but are not dead yet and many adults are dressed in black. Simon gets to Dreamtrue School and is confronted by a scene from a nightmare. All the students are dressed in black, they're all sitting around and either screaming or crying. Jilla runs up to Simon and says, "Simon, you're not dressed in black like the rest of them." Simon says, "No I haven't been infected yet and I see you aren't either." Jilla says, "Oh Simon what's happening?" Simon says, "I think I have an idea but Rino has to conclude the testing to prove my theory." Jilla says, "You still think this is all about the contaminated dirt?" Almont hovers up besides Simon and Jilla and says, "Are we the only ones still able to dream in all of Dreamville?" Simon says, "We need to find Rino and have him hurry his testing on that dirt. If it is the dirt than we have to prove that Miss DreamNot spread the black powder all over town." Just as Simon finishes saying this, Principal Toombs comes out of the school and says, "All right all you cry babies get to class." Everyone gets up and slowly go into the school. Simon and Almont park their hover bikes while Jilla waits for them. All three go into Dreamtrue School. Simon asks, "Where's Rino?" Jilla says, "I don't know. He didn't meet me this morning to walk to school." Almont asks, "Is that odd?" Jilla replies, "It's unusual for him. He's always prompt and on time." They walk into their musically inclined class to face a group of crying, angry, dreamless classmates. They throw their hand held computers at the three of them and unsuccessfully try to spit on them too. Almont says, "Let's get out of here before they get angrier and scarier." All three of them run out of the class and out of the school. Jilla says, "We have to get Rino out of the science inclined dreamers class." Almont says, "Um Jilla that won't be necessary. Have a look." Almont's hand held virtualcast, still functioning, shows the dream squad arresting Rino. Simon says, "Turn it up." The virtualcast clown reporter says, "This dark and not so dreamy morning in Dreamville, Rino DreamScifi has been arrested as the prime suspect behind the orchestration of dream stealing from Dreamvillians. His latest patented invention that filters or stops dreams has been confiscated from every house as the dream squad scientist tries to detect how he has set up his machine to fool Dreamvillians." Jilla says, "Look at him he's not dressed in black. He hasn't been infected." The virtual cast reporter says, "If Rino DreamScifi's proven to be guilty he will be banished for life from residing in Dreamville." Almont says, "What's he doing with his hands?" Jilla says, "He's a genius. He's using sign language to communicate a coded message." Simon asks, "What's sign language?" Jilla says, "It's a form of language used by a certain group of the population of the outside world." Almont asks, "Why would they need to develop a language using hand signals?" Jilla says, "Some of them are born without the ability to speak or hear. They'd have no voice or way of communicating without sign language." Simon says, "Interesting. What's he saying?" Jilla says, "I don't know." Simon says, "How's that going to help us then." Jilla says, "Quick we have to get to the ancient library with paperback books." Jilla gets onto Almont's hover bike and Simon gets on his and all three try to hover to the paper book library. Simon says, "Our hover bikes are infected." Jilla says, "Quick, we'll have to run through the back alleys so we don't get caught being out of class." They run in the direction of downtown Dreamville.

Once there, Almont's huffing and puffing, Simon's sweating and Jilla's cheeks are flushed with pink hues. Simon says, "Okay we're here. I'm guessing we'll have to sneak in here too." Jilla says, "You're right because we can't get caught here either." Almont says, "Everything's happening so fast." They sneak up to the side of the Paper Book Library and watch the dream squad security guard patrol up and down the front of the building. He comes right up to the side where they are but he doesn't see them in the bush. He turns around and walks back to the other end of the building and goes down that side of the building. Jilla whispers, "Quietly now, let's go." They get out of the bush and run up the steps into the Paper Book Library. They all hide behind a tall, large and wide statue of one of the ancient founders of Dreamville. They see the same security guard patrolling inside after entering through the back door and go back outside through the front door. Jilla whispers, "Okay, let's go, quick down on the floor." They crawl on all fours past the Librarians desk and into the rows and rows of book shelves with Paper Books. Jilla reads the signs and whispers, "Over here in this section of ancient forms of communication utilized by the outsiders. Keep quiet." Jilla stands up and pulls out a book from a top shelf. She opens it and starts reading. Simon reads over her shoulder and Almont keeps a lookout. Jilla whispers here, "Almont bring the virtualcast here and replay the part where Rino's using the sign language." Almont starts playing it but forgets to turn the volume off. The loud virtualcast alerts the librarian to their presence and she calls for the security guard. She says, "Guard, guard we have intruders in the Paper Book Library." Simon says, "Intruders?" Jilla says, "Yeah didn't I mention that this place is restricted."

Almont says, "No." Simon says, "Quick take the book and let's get out of here." Almont says, "This way there's a back door." They scramble to their feet and run out the back door as the security guard chases after them. "You three there, that book is restricted, you have to halt. Halt there in the name of the law." Simon, Almont and Jilla run as fast as they can losing the security guard when they duct into a large opening in the tree trunk of one of the ancient trees. Almont says, "I know this tree. My father has pictures of my great, great, great, great grandfather sitting inside this tree in his antique gasoline powered truck." Simon says, "We're running out of time. Jilla figure out the message from Rino." They walk out of the tree trunk and start to un-code the message. "Jilla says, "Okay look at his hand signal here, according to this book, he's saying; you have to finish, save me, I'm innocent, go to my lab, foreign substance, outsiders dirt, drop ancient motor oil, quickly." Almont says, "What are we supposed to conclude from that." Simon says, "We'll find out when we get there." Jilla says, "Boys back in the tree trunk." The security guard walks by and towards the Paper Book Library. Simon says, "Now, let's run to Rino's lab."

They successfully avoid the multiple dream squad police, investigators and security guards by not running through the streets, drives and back alleys. Instead, they walk from bush to bush and from tree trunk to tree trunk all the way to Rino's house. They hide in a bush just outside his house as the sun goes to sleep and the darkness of the night starts to creep around them. Simon says, "It looks like his parents aren't home. Let's go inside." They sneak up to the front door and Almont says, "Locked." Jilla signals to follow her around to the back door, she turns the knob, another locked door. Simon points at an open window. Almont says, "Jilla we'll hoist you up, once your inside, come and unlock this door" Jilla says, "It's the only idea we've got. Okay, hoist me up." They hoist her up and she falls inside the house on the hard floor. She exclaims, "Owe!" Simon asks, "Are you okay?" She gets up, walks to the back door, unlocks the back door and says, "Yeah I'll be fine." Almont and Simon walk inside and lock the door behind them. They quietly walk through the house, through the DreamScifi's garage and into Rino's science lab. Jilla says, "Look an antique battery powered flashlight." She turns it on for light. Simon says, "Good, at least we won't have just the moonlight as our only source of light." Almont says, "Yeah who knew Dreamville would ever be completely without light and powerless." Simon says, "Okay now Rino said to drop some ancient motor oil on the soil." Jilla asks, "What do you think we'll happen?" Simon says, "I don't know. All I know is we need to conclude his theory." Almont says, "Look he wrote it down in hand writing on a piece of paper."

The theory; I've recorded that Dreamville's soil never stains even with massive amounts of motor oil poured onto its surface. The oil simply evaporates. This is in concurrence with the findings of my reading in the ancient science book series labeled soils which leads me to believe that this black powder is foreign and from the outside world. To prove this, I will separate the two soils and pour the ancient motor oil on the black powdery substance, if it stains and makes the dirt stick together, this dirt is from the outside world." Simon says, "So that's what he was on the verge of proving." Jilla says, "Look, I'll read. Rino wrote; I have to note that these two soils together emit a strange wave that renders Dreamvillians technological tools that use computer chips absolutely mal-functional. These two soils combined together scramble the signals that computer chips need to operate our livelihoods such as our dream catchers. Therefore my forgone conclusion will be that the contact between these two soils causes a magnetic reaction wave which every scientist knows damages and destroys computer chips." Simon says, "That makes complete sense to me. Let's finish his experiment shall we." Jilla whispers, "Shush, his parents just got home." They can hear Rino's parents talking in the garage. Mrs. DreamScifi says, "It's not enough that no one's dreaming because of the real dream stealer but they have false accusations against our son. He's only fifteen and they want to banish him. I can only sympathize with the parents of those poor missing kids, Simon Dreamlee, Jilla MusiDream and Mayor AllDream's son." Mr. DreamScifi says, "Come now dear. There isn't much we can do standing around and crying. Let's go inside and consult with our Mr. DreamLaw, the best lawyer we know. First, I'll check Rino's science laboratory." They can see the door knob turning just as Mrs. DreamScifi says, "Dear, our lawyer's already here." Rino's father releases the door knob and they hear them open the door, go inside the house and shut the door. Simon looks at Jilla and says, "We better hurry or we'll get caught for sure."

Simon takes the already separated soils and places the black dust in front of him. Almont passes him the dropper with the motor oil inside of it and Simon drips it onto the dirt. They watch while nothing happens. Jilla says, "Put some more on." Simon nods his head in agreement and takes the oil can and pours it all on the identifiable black dirt. They watch as Almont writes down their observations. Simon says, "Look, the dirt is starting to stick together." Jilla says, "And the motor oil is leaving a stain in the dirt too." Almont says, "The first part of Rino's theory is right, now for the second part." Simon says, "Jilla get those other two flat tins over there and bring them here." Jilla reaches over and places them in front of Simon. He takes out his personalized computer chip sized computer and holds it over Dreamville's soil. Simon says, "Log on the Internet. It's functioning normally." Jilla holds hers over the black dirt and says, "Log onto the Internet. It's functioning normally." Simon takes the black dirt and puts it back into the Dreamville soil. Simon says, "Okay here it goes." He holds his computer over the soil and sure enough the signals are scrambling and his computer crashes. Jilla does the same and the same mal-functioning occurs. Almont says, "There we have it, Rino's theories are in fact right." Simon says okay, so we know that the dirt is from the outside world. Now we have to prove to everyone that the real culprit's Miss DreamNot and we'll have to do that by going into the forbidden wall of the forest and taking pictures. We have to do this tonight. We have to catch her spreading the outsider's dirt onto everyone's properties in Dreamville." Jilla says, "Agreed." Almont says, "Yeah agreed." Simon says, "Good we're all agreed then." Jilla says, "First, we should hide the evidence from the adults." They grab three tin canisters and put the dirt in the canister being careful not to re-mix the already separated soils.

They bring them with them as they quietly tip-toe out of the back door of the garage into the bushes. They travel the same way they got there from bush to bush and tree trunk to tree trunk. Jilla says, "Hide them in here, in the trunk of the ancient tree. It'll be easy to remember because it's the only one in front of Dreamtrue School." The boys nod their heads in agreement. Jilla tests the flashlight and it works fine. Jilla says, "We're going on foot?" Simon says, "We have no other choice." Almont gulps and says, "I hope none of the wild animals are hungry tonight." They walk down the forbidden road into the forbidden forest wall. Jilla grabs Almont's hand and loops her arm through Simon's arm as they stick to the centre of the dark road. Simon flashes the light of the flash light straight in front of them. They can see the glowing eyes of the forest animals along the either side of the road right up until they reach Miss DreamNot's shack. Her shack has a light on and Simon whispers, "We have to get closer." As he's about to move forward a wolf jumps in front of them, growls and bears his very sharp teeth. The wolf circles them, growling and howling. "Ahooo…" Almont says, "Quick, Simon, pick up and pass me that rock by your foot." Simon picks it up and Almont grabs it from his hand. Almont whips the rock at the wolf. The wolf yelps and runs away. They hear the rustling of a bunch of paws running in the same direction and howling. "Ahooo… Ahooo… Ahooo…" Almont says, "The wolf thinks the impact of the rock is a bullet from a hunter's gun." Jilla says, "Good thinking." Simon says, "Okay, shush, we have to get closer." He turns the flashlight off and now all they have is the light from the moon but unfortunately it's a cloudy night in the outside world.

They creep up to the dirty window and they look inside. The small one room shack and Simon says, "I don't see her. Do you?" Almont says, "No." Jilla says, "No I don't either." Simon says, "We have to go inside." They tiptoe around to the front of the house and Simon turns the door knob. They walk inside and into the small dirt shack. Once inside, Almont closes the door behind them. Simon says, "There, in that corner are half of the boxes of obsolete computer chips." Jilla asks, "Why did she steal old computer chips?" Simon says, "That's another clue we're here to solve." Almont asks, "Do you hear that sound?" They listen and hear knocking noises underneath the house, Simon says, "It sounds almost like the muffled voice of someone trying to cry for help." Jilla says, "Look a trap door. Should we go down there?" Jilla opens the door and the attempted cries are getting louder. Almont and Simon start going down the shaky stairs. Jilla follows behind them. Once all three are in the basement they're shocked by the discovery. Jilla says, "Miss LossDream?" Simon and Almont quickly untie her and Miss LossDream says, "Oh thank you, I was beginning to think that nobody noticed I was missing. She kidnapped me last night." Simon asks, "Where is she now?" Miss LossDream says, "I don't know. She said she had to complete what she started ten years ago." Almont asks, "Do you know what that might be?" Miss LossDream shakes her head and says, "No, not really." Jilla walks to the back of the basement and says, "Look what's this contraption?" Miss LossDream says, "I saw her use that to grind the obsolete computer chips into fine black dirt. She's the thief." Suddenly, Miss DreamNot says, "That's right missy. I grind the obsolete computer chips into fine black dirt and that's all it is." Simon says, "No it's not. I saw you spread it around Principal Toombs house and around Dreamvillians yards. It magnifies as soon as it comes in contact with Dreamville's soil and everything gets scrambled and all computer's with computer chips crash." Almont says, "Yeah so everyone's having their dreams stolen from them." Miss DreamNot laughs very eerily and just like the laugh they all heard after Simon's showing of his dream come true. "Ha-ha. Ha-ha. Aha. Aha." She pulls out a rifle and points it at Miss DreamNot, Simon and Almont. Jilla hides behind the empty boxes of obsolete computer chips. Miss DreamNot says, "Almont Alldream, the precious mayor's son, you will grab that rope over there and you will tie up Simon and Miss LossDream. Get moving." Almont picks up the rope and proceeds to tie them up. Miss DreamNot says, "Good job boy. Now over there bring me that extra rope." Almont picks up the rope and hands it over to Miss DreamNot and she says, "Turn around and face those two." She holds the gun against his back as she ties him up too. She walks to the back part of her basement and picks up a bucket of the finely grinded obsolete computer chips and mixes in the back dirt from her basement, she turns around and walks to the stairs. She says, "I guess that no one's going to find any of you now, not that they'll even care. Ha-ha! Aha!" She walks upstairs cackling and slams the trap door shut. They hear her lock the door, her footsteps on the creaky floor and hear her leave the shack. The sound of her hover car overpowers the wolves howling outside and then she's gone. Jilla comes out from hiding behind the empty boxes and says, "That was too close." Simon says, "Quick come untie us." Jilla runs up to them and unties them. Miss LossDream says, "What are we going to do? We can't walk through the forbidden forest." Simon says, "We have no choice. Quick, take pictures of the empty computer chip boxes, this grinding contraption, the dirt on her floor and the full computer chip boxes upstairs in the corner." Jilla says, "We're on it. We have no time to lose or else they'll banish Rino from Dreamville." All three of them start taking pictures of all the evidence in the basement while Miss LossDream tries to open the trap door. She says, "It's no use kids, this door is locked with an old fashioned hook of some kind." Almont looks at the small window and says, "Jilla are you ready to be hoisted out another window?" Jilla nods her head and Simon and Almont hoist her out the small window. They wait in the basement while Jilla makes her way to the front and through the front door. They hear a shattering crash and then silence. Simon yells, "Jilla!" Suddenly, they hear the lock of the trap door and see Jilla opening the trap door. Jilla says, "Sorry, I had to break a window to get inside. It scared the wolves away." They come upstairs and take pictures of the full boxes and of Miss DreamNot's shack. Jilla quickly goes in the basement to get the flashlight and comes back up and says, "Okay I have the flashlight. Let's go." Almont searches through Miss DreamNot's drawers and finds a padlock lock and says, "I have an idea. We'll lock her out of her own house." Simon asks, "How exactly are you going to do that without a tool of some kind?" Almont replies, "Oh yeah, I didn't think of that." Simon says, "Come on let's go." They exit the shack and are in the dim, cloud covered moonlight. Jilla turns on the flashlight. Jilla asks, "Which way do we go?" Miss LossDream says, "Straight ahead." Almont says, "I think this constitutes a nightmare come true." They walk out of Miss DreamNot's small opening for a yard and into the forbidden forest wall.

Once in the forbidden forest, they walk with a quick pace following Jilla. Jilla holds the flashlight straight ahead to see where they're walking, "Crack!" Jilla says, "What was that?" She flashes the light in the direction of the noise. Simon says, "It was nothing, just keep walking everyone." Almont says, "Look it's just a doe and her fawn." They walk some more in silence when they hear another loud sound, "Crack!" Miss LossDream says, "That's not the deer making that cracking sound. We better run.", "Crack!" Simon says, "Run!" They start running and Almont says, "Stay together if we get separated we won't have a chance to make it back to Dreamville. Jilla stops as her flashlight shines on a large grizzly bear. One by one they crash into each other and all stare at the grizzly bear. The bear roars loudly and Almont says, "We're standing between her and her cubs." Miss LossDream says, "Okay no one panic or we'll panic her." Jilla says, "Uh, Miss LossDream she's already panicked because she's a female bear and female bears will do anything to whatever gets between them and their cubs." Simon yells, "Run!" They start running sideways and then straight forward to try and get around the female bear. Almont screams, "Keep running, she's right behind us." They run and run and run until they're out of breath. They stop to catch their breath and Jilla remarks, "Look, morning, look the sun's getting up over mountain of dreams." Miss LossDream says, "Mountain of dreams, come children, Dreamville must be this way." They follow Miss LossDream down the slope that ends the forest wall and into the field behind the hill of Principal Toombs house. Looking behind them they see the bear and her cubs won't set foot past the edge of the forest wall. Simon says, "How did we end up way on the other side of Dreamville." Almont says, "I guess we were too focused on running to not get killed or eaten by the mother bear." Jilla says, "Boys Dreamville's so quiet and lifeless for a Saturday." They hear the cries of their neighbors and friends as they wake up from another dreamless night. "Ah… Ah… Ahhhhh… Ah…" Simon says, "They sound like they're in so much pain." Miss LossDream says, "They are. Imagine not dreaming. You can't because dreaming is a part of our heritage. It's what keeps us happy." Simon says, "No wonder Principal Toombs has been miserable for the past ten years. Every mean action he does, every mean comment and punishment he's ever said to people and imposed on kids are, entirely not his fault." Miss

LossDream starts to cry and hugs Simon and says, "Oh thank you Simon!" Miss LossDream starts to run towards Principal Toombs hill and up the hover way driveway. Almont says, "Miss LossDream where are you going?" Simon says, "No let her go Almont. My dream come true, it's about Miss LossDream and Principal Toombs." Jilla says, "And, Miss DreamNot's the evil, scorned third woman. Oh... how romantic! A real life love story with an evil twist in Dreamville, how dreamy." Almont says, "Not so much. We have to save Rino." Simon says, "Yes but first we have to catch Miss DreamNot and prove everything to the dream squad." Jilla says, "It almost sounds easier to break Rino out of prison so he can show the results to your father Simon or to the dream squad chief." Simon's eyes get big and round and he says, "Now that sounds like a plan. That deserves a high five." They all high five each other and head towards Dreamville's un-escapable prison.

Chapter Eleven – Fugitives

They walk through the barren streets of Dreamville listening to the agonizing cries and screams of the citizens of Dreamville. Almont says, "We have to hurry half the people have painted their houses black." Simon says, "There's no one outside. Not even the dream squad." All of sudden they hear the sound from the hole of a muffler, "Pow!" Jilla grabs their hands and says, "Hurry in here." They hide in one of the abandoned hover cars as Miss DreamNot hovers by sprinkling the black dust everywhere. Simon risks getting caught but manages to take pictures of her sprinkling the fine powder. Almont says, "Duct Simon." He pulls him down as she comes around again. She hovers outside of the abandoned hover car and says to herself, "Naw… They're securely tied in my basement." She gets out of her hover car, they hear her start walking towards the crashed hovering vehicle and Jilla whispers, "Get under this blanket guys." They quickly get under the blanket. Miss DreamNot looks into the hover car, satisfied there's nothing unusual, she climbs back into her hover car and hovers away. They get out from under the hot blanket and jump out of the abandoned hover car. Almont says, "Whoa… That was too close for comfort." Simon asks, "How is it her hover car still functions?" Jilla says, "By the sounds of it, her car has a muffler…" Simon finishes her sentence and says, "Which means her car doesn't run on solar power but by gasoline, the outsider's gasoline. That's it we need to expose her as living in the forbidden woods and then the adults will listen to our case against her." Almont says, "Case against her, you sound like you're going to court again." Simon says, "Hey, I had to go to court to fight for my dream to come true didn't I." Jilla says, "Boys, never mind that right now. Remember Rino? Focus on getting him out." They start walking in the direction of the Dreamville dream prison and sneak inside.

Once inside, they find no security guards and the dream squad isn't around either. They walk right up to Rino's prison cell. Rino stands up smiling. He too hasn't been affected by the powder and he says, "Jilla, I'm so happy to see you." Jilla and Rino give each other a kiss on the lips. Almont says, "Okay that's enough smooching. We have a mission to complete." Simon looks at the lock and says, "I still have my mother's hair pin in my pocket so I'll try it on this lock." Almont says, "This is a modern lock not an old fashioned lock like at Principal Toombs house." They hear a click as Simon successfully picks the lock and Rino comes running out. Rino says, "Thanks guys." Simon says, "Don't thank us yet thank the scrambled computer chips. The modern force field that usually surrounds this place is down. Never mind that right now, we have to find a way to clear your name and we need to act fast." Jilla says, "Yeah, people are even painting their houses black. Suddenly they hear the dream squad chief say, "Well, well, look at the missing threesome showing up to break out their friend. I should have suspected that you were all in cahoots." Jilla says, "No, no we're not. Rino's innocent sir." The chief says, "That's to be proven during his trial, until then, he's to remain in prison." The chief starts walking towards them with his hand gun pointed at them. Almont lunges at him, which confuses the chief and Simon trips the chief and yells, "Run Rino." They all run out of the Dreamville Dream prison and into the closest ancient tree's trunk to hide. The chief comes running out screaming, "Rino DreamScifi, you come back here. I promised your parents and their lawyer that you would be well protected in here. I can't protect you out there. Rino come back." They watch the chief who's also not infected run down the street in search of their foursome. Rino says, "Protection? I need protection from whom?" Jilla says, "You don't know? Rino when I said people are painting their houses black I should have said that everyone's infected with dreamlessness." Simon says, "Miss DreamNot has been spreading the black dust everywhere, all night long." Almont asks, "Why are we so special? Why aren't we infected?" Rino says, "Almont brings up a good point. What's the common denominator?" Simon says, "I didn't throw out my obsolete computer chip. I have it in my pocket." Almont, Jilla and Rino look at him as they all pull out their obsolete computer chips from their pockets too. Jilla says, "Rino Miss DreamNot stole all the obsolete computer chips to grind them up into the outsiders soil and that's the mixture she's spreading around Dreamville." Rino says, "So the yellowing of Principal Toombs eyes is because of breathing in the fine metal dust. Anyone's eyes would turn yellow. Our lungs aren't meant to filter out fine metal dust, plus, it would get directly in his eyes too." Simon says, "Yeah only now it's in everyone's lungs and eyes." Jilla says, "Quiet,

Miss DreamNot's hover car." "Pow... POW... Pow..." Rino whispers, "That sounds like a hole in a muffler." Simon hushes him, "Shush." They sit silently until she's driven by and no longer within ear shot of hearing them. Rino says, "Do you all realize that means her car runs on gasoline, outsider's gasoline?" Jilla says, "Yes we realized that." Simon says, "Now if we can get the Dream squad chief to realize this, he might also realize that she lives in the forbidden forest and not only that she leaves Dreamville when she's forbidden to do so." Rino says, "Not only that, it's illegal to have any gasoline operated machine in Dreamville." Almont says, "Quick we have to go get Miss LossDream. She knows everything and she can convince the dream squad chief to arrest Miss DreamNot." Simon says, "Good idea." Rino says, "So where are we going?" Jilla says, "Principal Toombs house." Rino says, "Principal Toombs?" Jilla says, "Yes Principal Toombs house." She grabs his hand and pulls him out of the tree trunk to follow Almont and Simon who have already started strategically maneuvering from bush to bush and ancient tree trunk to ancient tree trunk.

Half an hour later, Simon's pinned in an ancient tree trunk by Mrs. LandDream's Scottish terrier dog, Terrance. Simon tries to hush him, "Shush Terrance, shush." He's almost caught by Miss DreamNot as she hovers around the tree. She gets out and looks inside the tree. Jilla whispers to Rino, "Oh no, she's going to catch Simon." She comes out of the tree trunk and says, "Stupid dog, probably chasing your own tail hey." She climbs into her hover car and goes in the other direction. They all run to the tree trunk and Almont says, "Simon?" Simon drops down from the top of the tree trunk and says, "I'm right here!" Jilla says, "Okay we're almost there." Simon says, "Run? Everyone agrees we make a run for it, all the way up the hill to Principal Toombs house." They all smile at each other and give each other high fives. They start to run as fast as they can past Almont's house, past Simon's house and to the foot of the hill. Once they're all at the foot of the hill, together, they all start running up the steep incline of the hill. Once at the top they stop at the gate with the gargoyles. Rino says, "I've never been this close to his house. It's creepier than from far." Jilla says, "Especially with those statues of gargoyles and all the dead plants and trees." Simon says, "If we don't hurry, all the plants and trees including the ancients ones will be dead just like Principal Toombs yard." They walk up to the door and Simon knocks on the door. "Toc... Toc... Toc... " Rino asks, "Wait you're just going to knock on the door and expect him to let us go inside." Simon says, "Yes because Miss LossDream is here and she's explained everything to him by now." They hear Principal

Toombs footsteps coming to his front door. They all hold their breath as he turns the door knob and he opens his door. Principal Toombs says, "Ah I've been expecting you kids. Come in, come inside and find some places to sit." They all go inside and sit in his dusty chairs. Principal Toombs closes the door and says, "I hear, you have been up to a lot of stuff lately." Jilla asks, "Where's Miss LossDream?" Principal Toombs turns around to look at her and replies, "Oh she's been here. She told me quite a story about your little adventures, suspicions and accusations." Simon says, "It's all true Principal Toombs. We need you to tell us where she is now because we need her help." Principal Toombs says, "Oh is that so. What do you need her to do?" Jilla looks at the floor and spots a rope coming out from behind a closed door. She looks at Simon and with her eyes signals him to look in the direction of the rope on the floor. Simon sees it and says, "Principal Toombs what time did Miss LossDream leave?" Principal Toombs says, "I don't recollect when she left. I believe you were going to explain how she's to help you four." Simon quickly gets up and opens the door to find Miss LossDream tied up in the closet with a gag around her mouth so she can't scream. Rino quickly gets up and trips Principal Toombs on the floor. Almont and Rino get on his back with all their weight to pin him down and to keep him from getting up. Principal Toombs says, "Why you troublesome, meddlesome kids." Jilla unties Miss LossDream and asks, "Are you okay?" Miss LossDream says, "I'm fine now. Kids don't hurt him. Despite what you see and what he did there's good in this man." Simon throws the rope to Rino, Almont and Rino ties Principal Toombs and then they carry him to a chair. They sit him down in the chair.

Another half an hour later, Principal Toombs sits in the chair while Miss LossDream asks, "Did you guys break Rino out of prison?" Jilla replies, "Yes we did. He's innocent and we need as many uninfected people as possible to fight against Miss DreamNot." Simon says, "That's why we came back here Miss LossDream. We need you to talk to the dream squad chief. He'll listen to you. You're an adult." Miss LossDream says, "That I am. What do you want me to tell him?" Simon says, "First we need her behind bars so tell him that her hover car has a hole in the muffler therefore she's using illegal outsider's gasoline. After he arrests her and has her behind bars, we can present all the evidence." Principal Toombs asks, "Evidence what evidence?" Simon says, "Well Principal Toombs answer this question first; has it been ten years since you've dreamed and had any sort of dream come true?" Principal Toombs sits in his seat getting angry and angrily answers, "Why you little that's absolutely nonsense, none of your business…" Suddenly he chokes up and starts to cry with large streams of tears, "…how did you… how…why… is it that apparent?" Simon says, "Principal Toombs can you please answer the question." Teary eyed and visibly pained by having to speak of his secret he says, "Yes, yes Simon, it's absolutely true." Simon says, "It's because of Miss DreamNot." Miss LossDream says, "Explain to him how she did it and how she's responsible for everyone in Dreamville being dreamless now." He sits in his seat, looks at Simon and Principal Toombs says, "Please Simon, do explain to me how she does it. How does she steal my dreams?" Principal Toombs keeps sitting in his seat looking at Simon. His face's tear stained but inquisitive, even though his mood shifts from sadness to anger and back to sadness while Simon explains to him how Miss DreamNot successfully stole his dreams.

Simon starts explaining from the beginning, he says, "A week ago now, before our trial, I observed Miss DreamNot snooping around your house on the same night Miss LossDream was here…" Impatiently Principal Toombs says, "Yes, yes get on with it." Simon continues to say, "She was sneaking around and spreading a black powdery substance all over your yard." Principal Toombs asks, "And, what's this mysterious black powder?" Rino starts to explain, "I did some scientific testing of this strange substance that Simon collected from your yard…" Principal Toombs angrily says to Simon, "So you're not just a trouble maker but a snooper too." Jilla says, "Principal Toombs, please focus on what we're telling you." Principal Toombs replies, "Right, right, okay you did scientific testing. Continue Rino." Rino says, "My theory was simple; the black powdery substance was dirt from the outside world. I separated the dirt from Dreamville's soil and developed a hypothesis. If the dirt is in fact from the outside world, ancient motor oil will make it stick together and it will stain." Principal Toombs says, "Why are you stopping with your explanation. Continue." Rino says, "Well this is when I got arrested and accused of being the dream stealer. I'm now officially a fugitive waiting to be vindicated." While he struggles to try and free himself from the tight ropes around his wrists, Principal Toombs angrily says, "So you have nothing, no proof just crazy, over active kid's imaginations." Jilla says, "No not at all. Simon the results, tell him." Simon says, "Almont, Jilla and I finished Rino's experiment. We dropped the motor oil on the black powdery substance and it stuck together and stained." Almont says, "Proving Rino's theory to be right." Rino says, "This is why when the contact between Dreamville's soil and this black dirt with ground up obsolete computer chips creates a magnetic wave that scrambles computer chips rendering them mal-functional and even crashes our systems." Principal Toombs says, "You expect me to believe this speculation?" Simon says, "Principal Toombs I observed you through that hole in your wall over there crying and smashing your new dream catcher. You cannot deny that it's because you couldn't even get it to log onto your account." Principal Toombs starts to cry again and says, "I couldn't understand how it functioned at the store and didn't here. I thought for sure I was absolutely dreamless." Miss LossDream says, "I think it's safe to untie him now." Almont says, "First, we should all show him that our computer chip sized hand held computers are also scrambled." They all show him and Simon says, "You see because of Miss DreamNot everyone in Dreamville's unable to dream." Rino says, "She's the dream stealer." Miss LossDream unties Principal Toombs, hugs him and says, "That's what happened ten years ago." Stunningly, Principal Toombs affectionately hugs her back when suddenly a rifle shot makes a giant hole through his front door. "Caboum…" Jilla says, "It's Miss DreamNot." Principal Toombs says, "Quickly, everyone go down into the basement." Everyone runs down the stairs to his basement.

Once in the basement Principal Toombs lifts an old, faded and dusty red carpet to reveal a trap door. Principal Toombs says, "Everyone, climb down the ladder." Everyone climbs down the ladder. Principal Toombs goes last, closes the trap door and with a strategically placed string attached to the carpet and threaded through the trap door, he pulls the carpet over the trap door. He can hear Miss DreamNot walking on the basement floor. He freezes and waits for her to go back upstairs and he starts down the ladder. Jilla reaches the bottom of the long ladder and steps on a cement floor. With her flash light she sees an ancient light fixture switch and flicks it on. The lights come on. Rino steps onto the cement floor, then Almont, Simon and Miss LossDream. Almont asks, "What is this place." Rino says, "It's a laboratory!" Principal Toombs reaches the cement floor and says, "It's a laboratory all right. It was my father's secret haven away from public life. No one in Dreamville knows about this place. Of course you all know about it now." Jilla says, "Well this is all great but we can't stay in here." Principal Toombs says, "I'll show you all how we'll get out but you have to promise me that you'll never tell anyone about this place because I don't want the media clowns to find out about this laboratory." Rino says, "Sure." Almont says, "Okay." Jilla nods and says, "Fine." Simon says, "No problem." Miss LossDream says, "We're all agreed Principal Toombs." Principal Toombs says, "Thanks everyone. Okay this way." They walk down a long corridor with ancient painted portraits of what looks like royal families." Jilla says, "Principal Toombs, look at these people. Who are they?" Principal Toombs says, "Oh they're my relatives going as far back as year one." They all look at the pictures and Jilla says, "The ornate jewelry adorned in rubies, emeralds, diamonds, gold and silver, gold crowns encrusted with gems, velvet clothing with fur accents and elegant and serious demeanors of their body language and their facial expressions. These are royalty." Principal Toombs laughs nervously and says, "Ha-ha… Royalty, no, not at all, now, everyone follow along, this way now." Simon walks along and catches a glimpse of a room filled with the very jewels from the pictures and Almont, looking the opposite way catches a glimpse of the clothing in the pictures. They both say nothing. Simon whispers, "A lot of rooms along this tunnel." They reach a large room with multiple ladders and Principal Toombs says, "Okay everyone up this ladder." Simon asks, "How do you know which ladder to climb." Principal Toombs replies, "I don't. Do you have a better idea?" Miss LossDream says, "Well start climbing the ladder." Jilla leads the way, followed by Rino, Almont, Miss LossDream, Principal Toombs and Simon. Jilla reaches the trap door and opens it. Simon asks, "What's up there?" Jilla says, "I'm not sure." She climbs out, followed by Rino, Almont, Miss LossDream, Principal Toombs and Simon.

Simon climbs out of the trap door and is confronted with the dream squad and the dream squad chief. Rino's handcuffed and Miss LossDream and Principal Toombs are desperately pleading with the dream chief to release Rino. Miss Loss Dream says, "Chief you're making a big mistake." Principal Toombs says, "Un-cuff him now. He's innocent. You should be building a case against Miss DreamNot." Simon says, "Dream squad chief, you have to listen to them. Rino's innocent." The chief says, "Put him in the prison cell." They take Rino away and put him back in the cell. Almont, Jilla and Simon's parents walk into the Dreamville prison with relief on their faces. Simon's mom says, "Simon you're alright. You've been found." Jilla's mother says, "Jilla my girl. I'm happy you're now safe." Mayor Alldream says, "Almont, I thought you were a goner." Dream squad chief says, "Yes we knew you guys would show up sooner or later. We just didn't know that Principal Toombs and Miss LossDream were your kidnappers. Thank goodness for Miss DreamNot's help to crack this case." Simon says, "No, you have it completely wrong. Yesterday, Miss LossDream was kidnapped by Miss DreamNot and everyone's dreams are being stolen by Miss DreamNot not Rino." Simon's dad says, "Now Simon you've just survived a traumatic event. It's time to go home." The dream squad chief says, "Well not quite yet, Mr. Dreamlee, I still have to deal with the matter of these three breaking Rino out of prison. Cuff them, Principal Toombs and Miss LossDream." Jilla says, "No, this is all a big mistake. Miss DreamNot is the one stealing all your dreams." The dream squad cops bring them to the jail cell and put them in the cell with Rino. Simon's mother says, "Simon will be back with a lawyer." Mayor Alldream says, "Don't worry son, I have sway with the Dreamville judge." Jilla's parents say, "We love you Jilla. Everything will be fine." They all exit the prison cell section of the Dreamville dream squad station.

They all sit quietly on the hard cement bench against the back wall in the cell. After five minutes, their handcuffs dissolve. Jilla says, "I'm sorry. I'm sorry I didn't recognize where we were before climbing out." Almont says, "It's hopeless." Principal Toombs says, "We've lost." Miss LossDream says, "Look, outside, it's already night time." Almont, Jilla and Simon yawn and lie down on the cement bench. Rino sits and strokes Jilla's hair. Simon checks his pocket for the bobby pin and discovers it's gone. Rino says, "I don't remember there being a trap door in the floor." Principal Toombs says, "They're visible only when absolutely necessary, otherwise, no one can see them or even open them at all." Silence and darkness fills the tiny cell as Simon drifts into his dream. Tired, the others fall asleep along side of him. Simon's dream is all about the boy dancer in his dream already come true. Simon wakes up filled with hope and says, "Everyone wake up. Wake up. We can't give up, at least not like this." They all wake up and Almont says, "Oh what is it now?" He looks around him and says, "Crap, this is not a dream. We're really locked up in prison." Simon looks at Jilla and says, "Are you ready to be hoisted up to that window, jump down and come back inside the front of the building and steal the key from the guard?" Jilla says, "I'll do it." Almont asks, "What about the bobby pin in your pocket." Simon says, "I must have lost it when we ran through the forbidden wall of the forest." Jilla says, "I'll do it." Principal Toombs says, "Okay, Rino get on my shoulders." Rino says, "Okay I'm stable enough, Almont come up." Almont climbs on top of Rino. Almont says, "Come up Simon." Simon climbs up the shaky totem pole, reaches the top and climbs on Almont's shoulders. Simon looks down at Jilla and says, "Do you still want to do this?" Jilla smiles and starts climbing up the swaying Dreamvillian totem pole. Miss LossDream goes from side to side trying to prevent them from toppling over. Jilla reaches the top and stands on Simon's shoulders, she says, "Hold still." Almont says, "We're doing the best we can." Jilla pulls herself up on to the ledge of the window and whispers, "Great there's an ancient grape vine. I'm going to climb down the vine. See you all in a bit." Simon whispers, "Be careful." Just as she disappears out the window, they all crash to the cement floor. Almont says, "Owe." Simon says, "Ah..." Rino says, "Ouch." Principal Toombs fall was broken by Miss LossDream. They uncomfortably lie on top of each other face, to face. Miss LossDream gazes lovingly into his eyes. Principal Toombs quickly gets up, pulls her up with him, assumes the role of authoritative figure, and says, "Good job kids. Good job." Suddenly the guard wakes up and says, "Quiet down in there." They all sit on the cement bench and wait for Jilla to retrieve the key. They wait and they wait. Almont whispers, "She's been caught." Simon whispers, "No she hasn't. You have to give her time." Rino whispers, "Plus she has to wait for the night guard to fall back to sleep. Shush." Sitting in the pale moonlight streaming through the window into the cell they periodically look at each other as they hope for the best outcome possible. They all hear the awful sound from the hole in the muffler of Miss DreamNot's gasoline powered hover car passing by and they all cringe at the thought that Jilla's out there, outside alone. "Pow... POW... Pow..."

Chapter Twelve – The Escapees

In the moonlight, Jilla climbs down the ancient vine and sets her feet on the ground. "Pow…" Jilla whispers, "Miss DreamNot's holy muffler." She ducts in the bushes with withered to dark brown leaves. She looks at the leaves and whispers, "Oh, I have to hurry." She watches Miss DreamNot sprinkling the black dust as she hovers by. Smelling the gasoline fumes from her illegal hover car, Jilla covers her nose. Jilla ducts really low to the ground as Miss DreamNot flashes her hover car's lights right into the bush where she's hiding. Fortunately, the lights go just above Jilla so there's no way Miss DreamNot can see her. She hovers away cackling and yells, "Ha-Ha… I'm going to be queen. Aha…" Jilla whispers, "What does she mean by that?" She gets out of the bush and quickly makes her way to the front of the Dreamville dream squad station. She's about to open the front door when she hears Miss DreamNot hovering back towards the station. She hides behind another large statue of one of the ancients. She sits there stilly and quietly. Miss DreamNot flashes her lights all over the front of the building and then hovers away again. Jilla sees Miss DreamNot's safely far enough away from the building that she couldn't possibly see her enter the front door. Jilla gets up, comes out from behind the statue and slowly opens the front door. She knows that none of the surveillance cameras are functioning so she slowly tip-toes into the lobby area. The lobby's devoid of anything and anyone. Jilla tip-toes into the dream squad office past the six sleeping cops but she steps on a dried up withered leaf, the loud crackle and crunch of the leaf under the weight of her foot starts to wake them up. "Scrunch." The dream squad cops start mumbling in their sleep and one starts to open his eyes. Jilla jumps behind a large pot that used to have a beautiful tree growing out of it and bites her lip. The one cop gets up out of his chair and walks around the room but he doesn't spot her. He sits back down in his chair and he whispers, "Must be my imagination." She waits ten minutes before making any kind of movement. She looks at the cops and being sure that they're all sleeping, she starts to tip-toe into the area of the prison cells and where her friends are being wrongly held captive.

Once there, they all spot her and she holds her finger to her lips to indicate to them not to make any noise. Suddenly they hear the holy muffler of Miss DreamNot's hover car hovering by the prison again. Jilla watches the security guard with the holding cell keys toss and turn. Afraid that he'll wake up she freezes with no place to duct behind. She waits for him to stop moving around and to all their relief, he doesn't wake up. She looks at them and then looks at the guard. She slowly approaches the security guard's office on her tippy toes, enters inside, approaches the soundly sleeping guard and reaches for the key ring with all the keys. It's hanging on a hook of his belt around his waist. She loses her grip when the security guard turns and lies on top of the key ring and like clockwork Miss DreamNot hovers by with a gigantically loud boom coming from the ever growing hole in her muffler. "POW... POW..." Jilla watches the security guard opening his eyes. She quickly glides to the opposite side of his view. He scratches his forehead, yawns, closes his eyes and turns around to the other side just as Jilla glides to the opposite side of his view again. The key ring is again retrievable. She slowly grips the key ring and lifts it off of the hook. Slowly tip-toeing backwards from the sleeping security guard, she slowly closes the office door by holding onto the door knob and slowly turning it into its latch. They all watch her with smiles on their faces. She turns around and holds her finger to her lips to remind them not to make any noise. Jilla tip-toes to the holding cell door and she tries seven different keys before finding the right one. Each one makes echoing noise that concerns all of them but finally she clicks the lock and opens the holding cell door. They all come out of the cell and Rino hugs her, she hushes everyone, "Shush." Principal Toombs is the last one down the trap door and he closes the trap door making a slight noise, he doesn't realize this slight noise wakes up the squad guards. They all climb down the trap door down the ladder back into the tunnel.

Once in the tunnel, Jilla asks, "What now?" They hear the dream squad guards coming down the ladder. "Quickly move now, the chief will be miffed at us if we don't catch them." Principal Toombs says, "This way, follow me." They all follow him to a stone wall and he taps it three times. The stone wall opens and they all go inside. The stone wall closes behind them sealing them inside. Jilla says, "I left the flashlight in the cell." Principal Toombs says, "That's alright I'll turn the lights on." He claps his hands and the lights come on. They find themselves inside a windowless room with more amazingly ancient portraits, statues and hard cover books in ancient hand writing. Jilla picks up the books and reads the title, "The Royal Family of Dreamville; The DreamRoyals." Almont says, "Dreamville doesn't have a royal family?" Rino says, "It's probably a story book of some ancient one's dream come true." Principal Toombs turns to them and hushes them, "Shush." They all listen at the stone wall as the dream squad guards walk by. One guard says, "They're gone sir. We've lost them." Another voice says, "We have to get back to the surface and patrol the streets until we catch all of them." They all listen with their ears pressed against the stone wall, they hear their footsteps getting fainter and fainter and suddenly they don't hear them anymore at all. They lift their heads from the stone wall and look at Principal Toombs. Simon asks Principal Toombs, "How do you know about all these secret places." Principal Toombs says, "I don't know. I wish I could answer you." Miss LossDream says, "You have to remember. You have to be the one who remembers." Simon asks, "What does that mean?" Miss LossDream weeps and replies, "I can't explain why." Principal Toombs walks to the other side of the room and taps on that stone wall and another door opens. He signals them to follow him. They all follow him into this new room and the door shuts behind them. Jilla claps her hands and the lights come on just like in the first room." Jilla says, "Hey look curtains" She opens the curtains and reveals a large window overlooking snow capped mountains and a summery, plush, green valley in full summer bloom. Simon asks, "Where are we?" Miss LossDream asks, "Yeah where are we?" Principal Toombs says, "We're inside of Dream Mountain and this…. This is the window to the outside world. The ancients used this window to observe them, monitor them, study them and dream up ways to better their lives, stop their petty wars and fill their lives with love, friendship, family and happiness." Jilla says, "Look over there." Principal Toombs says, "That's called a city covered in snow. The bright lights fill the night time like stars. Of course they need those lights or else it would be too dark to see on cloudy nights." Rino says, "Look over there. What's that building?" Principal Toombs replies, "That building is just one of their many religious monuments of many different religious beliefs." Almont says, "The outside world doesn't seem so bad." Principal Toombs says, "It doesn't seem that way now, but the ancients have recorded terrible, brutalities performed at the hands of humans not only against animals but against their fellow humans. No it may not seem terrible but they still have a lot to learn about peace. In fact, if they weren't always fighting with each other and opened their minds, they would be able to see Dreamville." Simon says, "This is all very interesting and all but we have to save our own world right now. We have no peace here right now." Principal Toombs closes the red velvet curtains and says, "How do you propose we do that? The dream squad chief doesn't even want to listen to us." Simon replies, "We have to get them to follow us down the forbidden road to Miss DreamNot's shack. This way they'll arrest her for living in the forbidden forest wall." Almont says, "That just might work, besides, they're too dim to realize that she's hovering around in an illegal gasoline operated vehicle." Jilla turns to Principal Toombs and says, "How do we get out of here?" Principal Toombs says, "Via this wall. This wall will safely lead us to the ancient meeting grounds." He taps the wall and the stone wall opens. They all walk inside and the stone wall closes behind them. Simon claps his hands and the lights come on. Principal Toombs says, "Follow me, straight ahead." They follow him putting their faith in his decision.

Almont whispers to Simon, "Did you ever think that we would be voluntarily following Principal Toombs anywhere." Simon whispers, "No, I absolutely thought he was evil but Miss LossDream's faith in him has ignited my faith in him too." Jilla whispers, "Boys, we can all hear you." Principal Toombs says, "Don't worry Jilla, if I were any of you following me right now, I'd be astonished too by the unexpected surprise twist in these past couple of days events." They walk and walk, Almont says, "It seems like we've been walking forever." Principal Toombs says, "We're almost there. We have just a couple more steps more." They keep walking looking at the mirrors on the walls and the never ending portraits of royalty on the walls. Jilla says, "Have you all noticed, each portrait is getting older than the next as we walk further down this corridor." Rino says, "I have been noticing." Principal Toombs stops and looks at the most ancient and the very last portrait. The portrait is of a Royal couple, a king and a queen dressed in velvet blues adorned in blue sapphires and crowns filled with sparkling white diamonds. Principal Toombs says, "I don't know what to do here? I have to think." They all sigh in disbelief and sit on the cement floor that oddly enough is warm as opposed to cold. Principal Toombs stares at the picture with a perplexed look on his face. Miss LossDream sits beside him waiting for him to remember.

Jilla's stomach rumbles and she says, "Sorry. I'm a little hungry." Almont says, "I think we all are hungry." Simon looks closely at the portrait and can't help but see a remarkable resemblance between Miss LossDream and the woman in the portrait. He chooses not to say anything but is startled by Jilla who whispers, "I see it too, the similarity between them." Simon says, "It's probably nothing." Jilla and Simon sit back down when Principal Toombs says, "The future is our past." The portrait opens like a door and they all look at each other in amazement. Principal Toombs says, "Come on." They watch him step inside with Miss LossDream and they all follow one after the other. At first, they're in complete darkness and it seems as if they're stepping on air. Jilla says, "I don't feel anything under my feet." Simon says, "Me neither." Principal Toombs claps his hands and suddenly they are practically blinded by a whiter than white light. Jilla says, "I see the gold outline of an outdoor room. Simon says, "I see gold columns." Almont says, "I see golden gargoyles and golden angels." Rino says, "I see many of the same golden statues of the ancients that are all around Dreamville." Jilla says, "Look down." Simon says, "It's Dreamville." Almont says, "What's left of it." Principal Toombs says, "We're not really in the sky, the floor's a looking mirror that sees into the most troubled places in the world. It's an ancient technology that the ancient's mastered but after a council meeting decided it would be best to keep this technology and how it functions hidden from their descendants." Rino says, "I remember reading something about this in a scientific mythology book. It's believed that only a true royal descendent of the original ancient royals would know how to use and build this technology and use it for the greater good. I thought it was all a myth." Simon says, "According to what you're saying, Dreamville's the most troubled place on earth." Jilla says, "That's terrible. It's Dreamville." They keep walking towards the outdoor room. As they get closer, the light fades a little bit, enough so they don't half to squint anymore. They reach the ancient golden outdoor room adorned in gold, silver, diamonds, gargoyles, angels and ancient statues of the ancients. Gold benches are all over the room. Principal Toombs sits on a bench and Miss LossDream sits beside him. Simon says, "What's the purpose of being here? We're not accomplishing anything here? We have to go back?" Principal Toombs says, "The ancients came here to meditate and think in times of crisis." Jilla asks, "Have there been other times of crisis?" Principal Toombs says, "Yes, ten years ago but everything's hidden in the restricted books section of Dreamville's library." Simon asks, "We already know what happened ten years ago and that it's directly related to today's event and has and is being caused by Miss DreamNot." Principal Toombs says, "That's too simple a solution. There's something more to this story but what is it?" Jilla says, "That's it. We have to get to the library and look up what the Dreamville Historian recorded in those books. Maybe they'll be something in there that will help us stop and catch Miss DreamNot." Rino says, "Guys what about that golden book over there." They walk over to the book. They look at each other and Simon begins to read.

Simon says, "The title of this book is; The Great Escape. Dreamville has always been a peaceful, loving community nestled and hidden away from the outsiders. The royals have always been happy with this quaintness, closeness and secretiveness. The last is what enables them to truly help the outsiders solve their problems as they observe them through the window. Unfortunately, the one remaining royal and the true heir to the title of direct descendant of an ancient royal of Dreamville was not prepared for personal turmoil within his own circle which to the past ancient royals had never been an issue. This royal fell in love but inexplicably fell out of love and hid themselves away to never be seen again and escaping divine royal duties and responsibilities to the citizens." Almont says, "That's it. Why your dream that just came true is practically the same. All that's missing is the third woman." Jilla nudges Almont and directs him in the direction of Principal Toombs and Miss LossDream and says, "Simon look at them." Simon turns around and says, "I see them. This isn't about stealing dreams. It's about keeping the true royals from their rightful place as heirs to the throne." Jilla says, "That explains Miss DreamNot's comment last night. She screamed that she will be the queen." Almont says, "Who would have ever thought that Principal Toombs is the king of Dreamville?" Jilla says, "No it's Miss LossDream. She's the queen of Dreamville." Principal Toombs abruptly stands up and says, "Kids come here, our ride back to Dreamville has arrived." They run over to Principal Toombs and Miss LossDream and wait. Jilla says, "I see nothing." Rino says, "I don't see anything either." Suddenly a golden door materializes before them. Principal Toombs asks, "Where do you want to go kids?" Simon says, "What do you mean?" Principal Toombs says, "Oh Simon always with the questions. It's good to have an inquisitive mind. This door will open anywhere you want it too. All you have to do is tell it the exact location." Simon says, "Oh, okay. Open, inside the ancient tree in front of Dreamtrue School." As soon as Simon finishes his sentence, the door opens and they see the inside of the ancient tree. They all step into the door. Once they're all in the ancient tree, the door shuts. Simon asks, "What now. Does the door stay here?" Principal Toombs says, "The door will stay here as long as it's needed. It's safe, only those who know how to use it will be able to step through it. Those who don't will open the door and only see a useless door frame." Rino says, "Genius." Jilla says, "Okay Simon, so why here of all places?" Almont says, "Yeah, I mean we're only going to get put in prison again." Simon says, "The evidence from Principal Toombs yard and Rino's scientific results. Grab them and we're going to the dream squad chief to show him our proof." "Pow... Pow..." Jilla whispers, "Oh no, it's Miss DreamNot." Jilla and Rino quickly hide with the evidence behind the door. They can hear her talking with the dream squad chief, "The ancient tree trunks. It dawned on me that they can easily hide in them." The dream squad chief says, "Now Miss DreamNot we're on the case. Will you please go to your home?" They hear him galloping away on a horse. Almont whispers, "They're travelling by horse now." Almost before he could finish his sentence, Miss DreamNot is holding her shot gun on them and cackling. "Ha-ha... Aha... I knew I would find you trouble makers in one of these ancient tree trunks. Gather against that wall over there." Conveniently, she has a rope around her waist and she ties them up. Almont's eyes keep focusing on the door. Miss DreamNot says, "What's the matter with you boy. Is there something behind this door? Oh that's right that Jilla girl and that Rino boy are a part of this group of mischiefs. Are they behind the door?" She quickly opens the door. Jilla and Rino see Miss DreamNot looking right at them through the door, but, the most unusual thing happens, she cannot see them. Miss DreamNot leans into the doorway and her eyes are right in front of Jilla's but she doesn't see them. Simon looks at Principal Toombs and he winks. Miss DreamNot slams the door shut and says, "Well I'll be on the lookout for those two. In the meantime you four will come with me." They walk out of the ancient tree trunk as Miss DreamNot points her shotgun at them. Jilla quickly goes to see where she's leading them. Jilla whispers, "She's leading them into Dreamtrue School. Rino you have to get the evidence and present your proof to the Dream squad chief. I'm going to follow them." Rino says, "High five." Jilla gives him a hug and says, "Be careful." Rino takes off in the direction of Dreamville's Dream prison. Jilla watches Miss DreamNot force her friend at gunpoint inside the school.

Once in inside of Dreamtrue School, Miss DreamNot says, "Keep walking straight ahead to the gymnasium. Come on let's go." She keeps the gun pressed up against Simon's back. She says, "Quicker or Simon here will be shot. Now, none of you want to see him with a hole in his body and his guts all over the floor now do you?" Principal Toombs, Miss LossDream, Almont and Simon all walk silently. Miss LossDream says, "Toombs, open the door up there to let yourself and your new friends here in the gym." Principal Toombs presses his head against the door and uses his body to open the door. They all walk inside. Simon says, "You're never going to get away with this Miss DreamNot." Miss DreamNot says, "Oh you're still cocky hey. How is it that you still think that I'm not going to get away with taking over Dreamville when I already have done exactly that?" Simon replies, "Because the Dream squad chief will eventually catch on to your scheme." Miss DreamNot says, "Principal Toombs, stop walking." They all stop walking and Miss DreamNot walks in front of them holding the shotgun towards them and opens a trap door in the corner of the gymnasium floor. She laughs, "Ha-ha... Ha-ha... Aha. I will put these gags on you so you can't scream for help. Ha-ha. Get down there now." They all go down the steps to the school basement. Miss DreamNot yells, "Simon, enjoy the rest of your days starving to death. It's a fitting ending isn't. Oh and don't count on the dream squad chief ever helping you out. He's wrapped around my finger or should I say I stole his heart. Ha-ha. Aha." She slams the trap door shut.

Jilla runs to the front doors of Dreamtrue School to look inside and sees her force them into the gymnasium. She waits for a few minutes and sees her come out of the gymnasium. Jilla runs to the side of the school and observes Miss DreamNot walk to her hover car, climb in and hover down the forbidden road out of Dreamville. Jilla whispers, "She must be gone to get more black powder. She'll be gone awhile then." She runs to the front door and discovers it's locked. She looks around for a rock. Finally she finds one that's big enough. Jilla whispers, "Oh this is Rino and my rock." They carved their initials in the rock with a laser beam. She picks it up and carries it to the front door. She takes the rock and smashes it against the window. She carefully sticks her arm inside the door to unlock it. Jilla successfully broke into Dreamtrue School. Once inside, she walks the long corridor and into the gymnasium. She doesn't see her friends anywhere. She whispers, "This is odd. I know I saw her force them in here." She keeps whispering, "Almont, Simon... Miss LossDream... Principal Toombs... Where are you?" There's no sound just the creaking floor boards beneath her feet when she walks.

Simon, Almont, Miss LossDream and Principal Toombs are in the school basement and they hear Jilla's whispers upstairs. They can't respond because they've been gagged. Simon spots an old broomstick and walks the group to the broomstick. They trip over each other and fall but they finally stand back up and Simon, being the only one with his hands tied in front of him, grabs the broomstick. With his hands tied up he struggles to hit the ceiling with the stick. He hits it three times. Jilla whispers, "What was that?" She trips and falls flat on the trap door to the basement. She quickly opens it and goes down the basement. She sees them there. Jilla says, "Oh you guys are okay." She gives them all hugs and starts to untie them. One by one they untie their gags. Simon says, "Where's Rino?" Jilla says, "I stayed behind to rescue you guys and Rino went to the dream squad chief to present the proof." Almont says, "Good that's good." Simon says, "Where's Miss DreamNot?" Jilla replies, "I saw her hover down the forbidden road. I assume she's gone to get more black powder." Simon says, "Principal Toombs, Miss LossDream we need to get the two of you protected from Miss DreamNot." Miss LossDream says, "Just us? We all need protection from her dream stealing." Simon, Almont and Jilla look at each other realizing that the two of them have no idea who they really are. Simon says, "Call it a hunch." Almont says, "Come on. We need to get out of here before she comes back and honestly, I've been tied up in basements enough times this week." Simon says, "I agree, everyone upstairs." They all get to the gymnasium and follow Simon out the side door of the gymnasium. Outside, they see Miss DreamNot hovering back up the forbidden road. Almont says, "She's already back." Jilla says, "Quick duct behind these dead bushes." Almont says, "We're doomed without the use of our technology." Simon says, "No, we just need to use our heads." Almont says, "Our heads?" Jilla says, "He means our brains." Almont says, "Oh sure." Simons says, "You guys, it looks like she's coming back here." They watch her hover by and hear her park her hover car in front of the school. They also hear her scream, "You punks just don't get it do you. You're not going to destroy my plans." Jilla whispers, "I think she saw the broken glass. I had to break in the school to get you out." Simon whispers, "So she already knows that we've escaped. That's means we have to high tail it to the ancient tree trunk and use the door to go someplace else." Jilla says, "We should decide now where to go." They hear her screaming inside the school. Almont says, "Never mind that now, she's in the school, run to the door." They all get up and run to the door inside the ancient tree trunk.

Once inside the ancient tree trunk, Jilla asks, "Where to Simon?" Almont says, "Quick Simon make a decision, she's coming. Miss DreamNot is coming." Simon looks at the door. Jilla says, "Simon, decide now." Simon feeling pressured says, "Open to Principal Toombs house." The door opens and they all quickly step inside. Miss DreamNot gets to the door and turns the knob but the door dissolves right before her eyes. At Principal Toombs house, they all breathe a breath of relief. Jilla asks, "Why back here." Simon says, "Because this is where it all began and it's where it's going to end." Almont says, "I've lost count of how many times we've escaped but our luck is bound to run out soon. Not only that, but Miss DreamNot heard you say Principal Toombs house so it's only a matter of time before she gets here." Simon says, "Well then we'll have to be prepared for when she gets here." Simon says, "Here's the plan. When we were in the hidden laboratory, I saw an old battery run tape recorder. We'll use that to record Miss DreamNot's confession. Her confession about what she did ten years ago and what she's doing now. We'll set up the old battery powered megaphone that I also saw down there and broadcast her confession to all of Dreamville." Almont says, "Alright, I'm on it." He runs down to the basement and down the trap door. Simon says, "Principal Toombs and Miss LossDream, you two are going to go and wait upstairs in the room and make sure to lock the door." They go upstairs and they lock the door. Jilla and Simon are alone waiting for Almont to come back. Jilla says, "Do you really think this will work?" Simon says, "For as long as the batteries do." Jilla says, "That's not what I mean. I mean are us little kids really going to defeat an adult?" Simon says, "In this case, we have to defeat her or we'll never ever know Dreamville the way it used to be ever again. We have to do it for Dreamville." Jilla says, "I get it, it's not about us or even Principal Toombs or Miss LossDream but for the idealistic dream filled notion the ancient royals used when they founded Dreamville." Simon says, "Or to put it simply, happiness. We're doing this to bring happiness back to everyone." Almont comes out of the basement and says, "We're in luck, the tape recorder and the megaphone work. There's even a tape in the tape recorder." Simon says, "Great, we'll set it up over here behind this ratty chaise on this table. The megaphone will be pointed towards Dreamville." Jilla says, "Oh, I hope this works." Simon says, "We all hope it works." Almont says, "So what do we do now?" Simon says, "We wait." Jilla says, "The door isn't disappearing." Simon says, "Remember what Principal Toombs said. The door will stay as long as we need it." Jilla nods her head. They sit at three different windows looking out each side to try and spot Miss DreamNot coming towards the hill and up the hill to Principal Toombs house. They can hear the "Pow... Pow..." of her muffler but they don't see her anywhere. Almont says, "She could be anywhere down there." Simon says, "Be patient. She'll come." Silently, they sit and wait.

Chapter Thirteen- Rino Has Difficulty Presenting His Evidence

In the meantime, Sunday afternoon, Rino manages to make it to the Dreamville dream squad station but no one's there. He looks around in every room and no one's around. He sits in the lobby and waits for one of the guards or the dream squad chief himself. He sits and waits. He hears Miss DreamNot's damaged muffler in the distance. "Pow... POW... Pow..." Upon hearing it come closer to the station, he walks around to the back of the desk and hides himself and the evidence under the desk. He whispers, "Where are all the cops, security guards and the dream squad chief? I don't have time to wait for them. Worse, Dreamville doesn't have time to wait for them either." He hears the front door open and listens to hear who it is. Miss DreamNot yells, "Dream squad chief, where are you, you incompetent?" Rino concentrates on not making any sudden movements or sounds." Miss DreamNot looks in every room and even right behind the desks but she doesn't bend over far enough to see Rino hiding underneath. He holds his breath. She walks around the desk to the front and straight out the front door. Rino can feel a bead of sweat rolling down his forehead. He exhales and whispers, "I have to get arrested again. It's the only way to get to present my case." He listens for her cracked muffler as she starts to hover. She hovers away and he finally doesn't hear the irritating sound of her muffler anymore. He leaves the evidence under the desk and crawls out from under it. He stands up and looks around at the bare office. He sees a blanket in the dream squad chief's office and goes in to take the blanket. He whispers, "I'll use this to hide the evidence while I go out to get arrested." He takes the blanket and drapes it over the evidence leaving it under the desk. He walks out the front door to try and find a security guard, dream squad cop or the dream squad chief himself.

Outside, he sees the trees are just about completely dead, the browning grass and the town is devoid of people like a ghost town. No one's outside of their houses enjoying the sunshine. He can hear dogs barking wanting to be taken outside for walks. He sees cats prowling around, jumping in and out of un-kept garbage cans but he doesn't hear any birds. The birds look like they've all left Dreamville for the outside world where the trees are still alive and green. He walks down the steps of the Dreamville Prison and listens for any signs of the dream squad crew. He hears nothing but the loud sounding muffler in the distance. "Pow…" He listens for the hoofs of the horses but hears nothing. The town is dead silent, abandoned, devoid of happy sounds and dreams coming true. Rino whispers, "I'm in a nightmare. This is a nightmare. I want to wake up. Wake up now. Okay, Rino get yourself together and focus on what you need to get done. Where are you, dream squad?" He walks off the steps onto the pavement and walks up Main Street of Dreamville. He looks in all the dreams become true shops and sees nobody and nothing but hand written closed signs. All the street lights have been scrambled and have crashed. Malfunctioning hover cars, hover bikes, hover trucks, hover vans, hover semis, hover buses, hover boards are littering everywhere. Crashed hover media clowns, crashed hovering virtual newscasters are also littering the streets. People's drapes are drawn in their houses to keep out the sun and the houses are all painted black. All things that used to be shining and polished are now dusty and dirty because the cleaning robots have also crashed. The Dreamville banks are closed and curtains drawn as well. He walks past his house and sees that it is still white which means his parents have not been infected. He contemplates going inside to see them. He whispers, "I should at least let them know that I'm okay." He goes inside his house but there's no one there. He whispers, "They must still be in secret meetings trying to figure out what's causing people to lose their dreams. Damn it, I should have told them what I know. If I could, only, get that moment back? That could be another invention. I could invent some kind of go back to that moment machine." He stops to listen as he hears Miss DreamNot hover by his house. "Pow… POW… Pow…" He covers his nose to not smell the gasoline fumes. He waits for her to go by until he no longer hears her hover car. He whispers, "I'll get caught by her before I get arrested by the proper authorities, if I'm not vigilant." His stomach rumbles and he decides to go the kitchen and eat before going to find the dream squad. He opens the cupboards which are bare. He opens the pantry which is bare and he opens the fridge. In the fridge are a few couple day old apples, oranges grapes, carrots, tomatoes, lettuce and peppers, bread, a few pieces of pumpkin pie and four chocolate bars. He grabs two chocolate bars and puts them in his pocket. He eats one of the pumpkin pies. He pets and feeds his dog, Snookers, and his cat, Whiskers, feeds his fish, Scales, feeds his bird, Chirpy. Feeling refreshed, he starts his quest to find the dream squad again.   He whispers, "I have to go gang. I'll be home soon and everything we'll be back to normal." He walks out the front door, down his driveway and onto the streets searching for the Dreamville dream squad but he still sees and hears nothing. He whispers, "This is ridiculous. Where could they be? I can't yell out come and get me because the way things are right now, Miss DreamNot will come instead of them and I have no idea what she'd do to me." He sits down on a corner bench and waits. While Rino waits, Jilla, Simon, and Almont also wait patiently in Principal Toombs house. They wait to execute their plan to expose Miss DreamNot for the evil plotter that she has convinced the adult Dreamvillians that she's not. Everyone's patiently waiting for something to happen but no one quite knows what that something is yet. They all know what they want to happen but it isn't working out in their favor.

While Rino sits on the corner bench, he notices people opening their curtains slightly to see who's sitting on the bench but they quickly close the curtains once they've seen him. Rino whispers, "They're scared of the outside world. Dreamville has turned into the outside world. How one woman, a fellow Dreamvillian, can be so evil and do this to us is unfathomable? It's just not cool. I have to put a stop to this madness. I just have to find those men in uniform." Rino stands up and starts running non-stop until he loses his breath. He gets disoriented and faints. Rino lies motionless on the cement in the middle of the street. From a distance, the faint sounds of Miss DreamNot's irritatingly loud muffler approaches. "Pow... Pow..." She hovers towards Rino's bay while she spreads the black dust cruelly and gleefully as she sings a tune she invented.

> No one dreams,
> No one dreams,
> No one smiles,
> No one smiles,
> Dreams won't come true.
> Dreams won't come true.
> No one dreams,
> No one dreams,

No one's happy,
No one's happy,
Dreams don't come true.
Dreams don't come true.
No one dreams,
No one dreams,
You obey me,
You obey me,
I'm the queen come true.
I'm your queen come true.
No need for your dreams.
My wishes are your lives now.
No dreams,
No dreams,
Ha-ha…
Aha…
Dreams don't come true.

Rino wakes to this terrible song and sees her hovering by. If he risks it, she will see him for sure, chase him and perhaps catch him. He doesn't have enough time to get up, run and hide. He opts to lie stilly with the hope she doesn't see him lying in the middle of the street. Miss DreamNot's too busy singing and sprinkling the dust to notice him lying on the street as she passes it by and doesn't turn down the street. He lies stilly listening for her muffler to grow fainter. Once it does fade and he no longer can hear it at all he sits up. He looks around him and down at his clothes. He's covered in the black dust. He gets up and dusts himself off. He looks around again and sees the peering eyes of some of the citizens of Dreamville as they look out their windows. Rino yells, "Come out, come out of your houses and fight her. We have to fight together. Come outside." He observes as they all one by one shut their curtains. He yells, "You cowards. You're Dreamvillians and Dreamville's under attack. We must band together and fight her." One man that Rino doesn't recognize opens his window and pokes his head outside. Rino asks, "Mr. DreamsAlot, is that you?" The man replies, "Yes Rino. Rino go home and quit disturbing us. We can't win." Rino says, "But we can, join me." Mr. DreamsAlot yells, "Life's not a dream Rino. Leave us alone." He slams the window shut and draws the curtains to block out the sun. Rino runs to his front door and bangs on the door. Rino yells, "Mr. DreamsAlot, open your door, open your door.

There's always hope. There's always hope." He backs away from the door when he realizes that Mr. DreamsAlot won't open his door. Rino runs down the back alley and in the direction of the dream squad station. He runs and runs, upstairs into the station that still remains empty. He yells "Where are Dreamville's finest?" He runs out of the station and into the streets again. He looks at the ground and says, "Horse poop and it's fresh." He decides to follow the horse poop trail. As he walks, he holds his nose, he avoids stepping into the fresh piles of poop, he whispers, "Beautiful and magnificent animals but it's too bad they're so messy and stinky." He follows the trail to no avail. The horses stopped pooping. He looks around at the earth under his feet and says, "I'm in a surrounding field." He looks at the dead crop of corn and then he sees multiple horses' hooves prints in the dirt. He follows them until he reaches the edge of Dreamville and the beginning of the forbidden forest wall. Rino says, "What's this?" The dream squad chief, the entire dream squad, his parents, Simon's parents, Almont's parents and Jilla's parents have built themselves a shelter. Rino observes them for awhile before revealing his presence.

He observes his father and Simon's father discussing passionately but he can't make out what they're saying. Rino whispers, "Simon's dad's infected but nobody else there has been infected." He looks at Jilla's parents consoling Mrs. Dreamlee and his mother's sitting quietly with Mayor Alldream and his wife. Rino whispers, "I have to risk it. I have to turn myself in to the dream squad chief." Rino sits down and holds his breath. He breathes again and exhales. He's not quite ready yet to do what he has no choice but do. He's ready when he hears the faint terrible singing of the terribly worded victory song of Mrs. DreamNot. He looks back across the field at Dreamville and makes the toughest decision he's ever had to make in his entire life. He gets up, stands tall and yells, "Here I am. Come and get me dream squad chief." Simon's mom yells, "No son. Don't." The dream squad chief yells, "Go on boys, go and get him." The dream squad mounts their horses and start moving straight towards Rino. Like he's been frozen in place, Rino doesn't move. He watches the dream squad chief and his dream squad cops approach him on their galloping horses. They start to slow down when they noticed that he's not running away from them and they stop. The dream squad chief gets off of his stallion and walks towards Rino. The dream squad chief says, "You have the right to remain silent. Any words you may use could and can be used against you in the Dreamville trials to be held against you." Rino holds his hands out to be cuffed. The dream squad chief cuffs his hands and they get him up on the stallion. Rino can hear his mother in the background crying and yelling, "He's innocent. He's innocent." The chief mounts the stallion too and they gallop back to Dreamville towards the Dreamville dream prison. While galloping, the dream squad chief says, "It's a good thing you turning yourself in Rino." Rino asks, "Is that the only reason you're patrolling the edge where Dreamville and the forbidden forest wall begin?" The dream squad chief replies, "I'll be asking the questions Rino." Rino says, "You'll never catch the others you know. They're too sneaky for you." The dream squad chief says, "They'll have to sleep, eat, drink sometime and when they do we'll be there to catch them. Plus, I doubt they can stay away from their parents forever." The dream chief yells, "Whoa!" They've stopped in front of the squad's station and the chief, his squad members and Rino get off the horse. Rino says, "Look around you. Everything's dead. The town is devoid of any signs of life because everyone's confined themselves inside their homes. There's the banging sound of Miss DreamNot's muffler in the distance and if she were closer you would here her singing her victory song about how she fooled all of us Dreamvillians. Chief you have to listen to what I'm saying to you." The chief grabs his arms and says, "Come inside now. Your jail cell's waiting for you and we'll take down your confession." Rino says, "You mean my vindication." The chief tugs at Rino as he guides inside the dream squad police station. They walk up the steps and just as one of the dream squad cops is about to open the door, Rino points out again, "Chief, look at the black dust on the ground that's a potent and important clue in this case." The chief pushes him inside the station.

Once they're all inside the station, Rino asks, "Where's my mother?" The dream squad chief replies, "She's safe with the other uninfected people. My dream squad security guards are there to keep them out of harm's way." Rino says, "You mean to keep me and the others away from them." The chief sits Rino down and says, "Sit still while I book you again." Rino says, "I have evidence to prove to you all that the black dust is dirt from the outside world with the grounded up stolen obsolete computer chips." The chief asks, "Yeah so what does this dirt do?" Rino says, "Mrs. DreamNot illegally lives in the forbidden forest wall and she grinds up the chips into the dirt from her basement and transports it into Dreamville. She then spread it all over the soil here in Dreamville." The chief's growing impatient says, "Yes, okay, get on with it now." Rino continues to say, "The contact between the outside world dirt and Dreamville's soil creates a magnetic wave. This magnetic wave scrambles our technology and is the cause of the computers crashing and the dreamlessness that we're all experiencing." The chief's eager to believe him and asks, "Where's this proof of yours Rino?" Rino looks at the main desk and says, "I hid it under a blanket under the main desk over there. Look under it and you'll see the evidence from the results of my scientific experimentations." The chief says, "Alright boys go check under the desk over there and bring me over what you find." The chief says, "Dreams help you Rino. You better be telling the truth." The dream squad cops come back and say, "Sorry chief but there's nothing under there." Rino exclaims, "What? That can't be? That's exactly where I left the evidence. Someone stole it. Mrs. DreamNot stole it." The chief says, "I'm sorry to have to do this Rino but you're going back in the jail cell." Rino says, "Wait, I can recreate the experiment under your supervision of course. I just need to collect the soil from outside and have access to my laboratory." One of the dream squad cops pleads with the chief, "Sir, I think we should let him at least try to prove his innocence." The chief says, "You're right but I will supervise him this time so he doesn't try and pull any funny business again and escape." Rino stands up, smiles and says, "You won't regret your decision dream squad chief." They walk outside, Rino's hands are still tied up, the chief helps him mount the stallion and then he mounts the stallion himself. They gallop through the streets to Rino's house. While galloping Rino only hears the horse's hooves but doesn't hear Mrs. DreamNot's busted muffler. "Clip… Clop… Clippity… clop…" Rino says, "Miss DreamNot must be gone to collect more of outsider's dirt." The dream chief yells, "Whoa!" The horse stops galloping and trots up the DreamScifi's driveway. The chief gets off and Rino slides off the horse. He asks, "Chief, my hands?" The chief looks at him and takes the cuffs off. Rino walks to the front door and the chief follows behind him.

Once inside, Rino goes to the kitchen to get some metal containers and a large spoon to use as a shovel. They go outside and Rino fills the containers with the contaminated dirt and they walk back inside. Rino carrying the two containers directs the chief through the garage to his laboratory. Rino re-creates his experimental testing of the soil. He says, "First I need that strainer over there. Please pass it to me chief." The chief picks it up looks at it and says, "Both soils are just going to filter through this." Rino says, "You would think so wouldn't you but outsider's dirt is coarse and thick while Dreamville's soil is extremely refined and fine. So Dreamville's soil just filters right through but the outsider's dirt stays in the strainer." The chief's intrigued by the filtering and separation process. Once Rino separates the two kinds of soils from one and other, he takes the ancient motor oil and starts to pour it on the black powdery dirt. The chief asks, "What is the oil supposed to prove?" Rino says, "Watch as the black dirt starts to stick together and stains." The chief says, "Right and this proves what?" Rino says, "Dreamville's soil doesn't stain and this ancient oil just evaporates upon contact but this black dirt, absorbs the oil, sticks together and is stained by the oil. This proves this is outsider's dirt as per every science book in Dreamville." The chief says, "Okay this doesn't prove that it's the source of everyone's dreams being stolen?" Rino replies, "No but this will. Here's my hand held computer chip sized computer, I'll hold it over Dreamville's soil." The chief says, "Well look at that. It's functioning properly." Rino says, "Now I'll hold it over the outsider's dirt. Watch while it still functions properly." The chief says, "Okay, I'm listening, you have my full attention." Rino picks up the other container of un-separated soils and pours that into a third container. He holds his hand held computer over the mixed soils and they both observe the hand held computer chip sized computer's signal being scrambled and eventually crash. Rino looks at the chief and the dream squad chief says, "So Dreamville's soil is contaminated with outsider's dirt." Rino says, "All we have to do is clean it up and haul it out of here." The chief says, "Easier said than done. No one's allowed out of Dreamville but the designated one." Rino says, "I think this situation calls for a little tolerance in regards to the ancients rule regarding the forbidden road sir, chief." The chief says, "You say that Miss DreamNot lives in the forbidden forest wall. This means I have to arrest her." Rino says, "She's also driving an illegal gasoline run hover car. You can arrest her for that too and then I can test her finger tips and under her nails for the outsider's dirt and once I find it you'll have enough proof to charge her and have her banned from Dreamville." The dream squad chief reacts sadly, "Banned from Dreamville." They silently look at each other contemplating what to do next when they hear something strange. Rino says, "What's that sound?" They run outside and stand in the driveway trying to locate the sound. "Caboum…" The chief says, "That was gun shots." Rino says, "It's coming from Principal Toombs house." Rino runs towards the hill and the chief mounts his horse. He starts galloping towards the dream squad station. He says, "Rino I'll be back with the dream squad police." Rino hears him but doesn't look back as he runs.

Chapter Fourteen – Simon Reveals the Truth

The same Sunday, in the meantime, in Principal Toombs media room, Almont's looking out the hole in Principal Toombs front door. They can hear Miss DreamNot's clanging muffler as she speedily hovers up the hill. "Pow… POW… Pow…" Jilla says, "Miss DreamNot's coming up the hill." Simon says, "Everyone clear about the plan." Jilla says, "I am." Almont says, "I am three. Get it three, because there are three of us." Simon says, "Great but there's no time for a sense of humor right now. Duct and hide behind your piece of furniture." Simon pulls a piece of thin string just a few feet from the door. They sit and wait. Suddenly, Miss DreamNot shoots her gun in the air three times. "Caboum… Caboum… Caboum…" She laughs, "Ha-ha… Aha… Ha-ha…" She walks up the steps and kicks the door open. She says, "Are you punks in here?" Almont clicks on the megaphone and the tape recorder. Miss DreamNot asks, "What was that?" She shoots at the tattered chair. "Caboum…" Her gunshot takes the back of the high back chair completely off. It falls on top of Almont who's lying flat on his belly on the floor but she still can't see him. She points her gun down at the floor and it catches the string. Miss DreamNot says, "What's this? Is it a hovering piece of string? I don't think so. But, where do you lead?" She pulls the string and Simon pulls it to keep it in place even though he realizes that his plan to trip her and get her disorientated as soon as she comes in is severely failing. She follows the string and Simon knows she'll find him because there's no way he can move anywhere without being heard and seen. Following the string to behind the sofa, she sees Simon sitting there pulling the string. He looks up at her as she raises her gun to his face. Miss DreamNot says, "Simon Dreamlee, I should kill you now. No one would even care." Simon says, "Kill, you want to kill me now?" Miss DreamNot says, "You aren't infected and by this time you should be.

You and all those who aren't infected will have to be killed in order for me to rule Dreamville." Simon says, "You're never going to rule Dreamville." Miss DreamNot says, "I already do rule don't I. No one's going to stop me are they? Certainly not you and your friends, one by one I'll kill them all and rule the rest. Ha-ha. Aha."   She shoots the wall behind Simon. "Caboum…" Jilla jumps out from her hiding place and screams, "Simon!" Almont stands up. Miss DreamNot laughs and says, "Ha-ha. Aha. You see what good does caring do when it will only get you killed. Your little friends will learn this lesson very soon. Stand over there you twerps." Almont and Jilla stand together in the corner by the basement door. Simon gets up from behind the couch and courageously walks over to the tape recorder and megaphone cleverly hidden under the table beneath the open window." Miss DreamNot says, "You have some nerve kid." Simon asks, "Why do I have some nerve. Is it because I'm going to expose you for who you really are?" Miss DreamNot says, "You don't have the intelligence to…" Simon says, "To what? To explain to you that I know that you are the third woman in my dream come true and that Principal Toombs and Miss LossDream are the two lovers whose true love you temporarily interrupted." Miss DreamNot yells, "TEMPORARILY… Temporarily interrupted, I destroyed it. They're never going to love or be happy again." Simon asks, "Why Miss DreamNot? Why are you so adamant about keeping them apart?" Miss DreamNot replies, "Oh so you don't really know anything do you? You're just trying to make me tell you. Maybe you're cleverer than I thought." Simon says, "Thank you. I'll take that as a compliment." Miss DreamNot says, "Compliment. That was an insult shorty. Haven't you ever heard sarcasm before?" Simon says, "Miss DreamNot, I accept it as a compliment because I do know more than you think I do." Miss DreamNot says, "Is that so, well Simon, do explain to me what you think you know." Simon says, "I know that ten years ago you successfully kept Miss LossDream and Principal Toombs from being together by stealing Principal Toombs dreams. At first you took his computer chip so he couldn't record his dreams and couldn't have them come true but that didn't stop his love for Miss LossDream. All he did was get a new computer chip. Still happy, he never noticed you and your growing obsession with him. Your jealousy of their love was so deeply profound that you had to move out of Dreamville and this is why you live in the shack in the forbidden wall of the forest. You've lived there for the past ten years stewing in your jealousy but you reveled in how miserable you made Principal Toombs after you discovered one night that the outsider's dirt on the bottom of your shoe and the Dreamville soil combined together scrambles computer chips causing them to crash. So ten years ago you spread it all over Principal Toombs Yard causing his new computer chip to get scrambled and crash and any new one's that he bought scrambled and crashed as well. In conclusion, this made him believe he was dreamless. Not only that but he believed it was his punishment for falling in love with a common Dreamvillian with common dreams and not a woman of ancient royal descent such as yourself." Jilla gasps and Almont says, "What?" All of a sudden Principal Toombs walks in the room from upstairs. Principal Toombs says, "Is this true Miss DreamNot? Could this boy be telling the truth?" Simon says, "Yes, Principal Toombs you know all about the hidden pathways, tunnels, the ancient grounds and portraits of the ancient royals and the secret codes to get in the hidden rooms because of your repressed memories." Miss LossDream walks in and says, "Remember Principal Toombs. You have to be the one to remember." Miss DreamNot points the gun at Miss LossDream and Principal Toombs stands in front of the gun and says, "To kill her you must kill me first." Simon says, "We all know you don't want to kill Principal Toombs, your love, your future." Miss DreamNot says, "No, I certainly do not." Almont says, "Then lower your gun Miss DreamNot." She lowers her gun as she slowly approaches Jilla. She pulls Jilla against her and holds the gun to her head. Miss DreamNot says, "I'll kill Jilla if you don't give me Miss LossDream." Simon says, "Go ahead. No one here cares about Jilla." Miss DreamNot looks at all their faces and says, "Liar. Quit fibbing. You all care about Jilla." Simon says, "No, no we don't. Go ahead shoot her." None of them speak as they follow Simon's lead. Simon says, "Aren't you going to shoot her." Miss DreamNot says, "What's the use, you don't care about her, besides, Miss LossDream should be the one dead. She should have been dead ten years ago." Principal Toombs says, "Ironically, she was dead. She was dead to me." Miss DreamNot says, "Why didn't she stay that way?" Simon says, "Because of my dream, my latest dream that just came true. It's about this saga. Miss LossDream recognized her life in the story I told and so did you. It bothered you that Miss LossDream dared to speak to Principal Toombs and worst came here to his house to beg him to try and remember what happened ten years ago." Principal Toombs says, "Simon saw you Miss DreamNot. He saw you spreading the outsider's dirt all around my yard. It was on the same night Miss LossDream was here with me." Miss DreamNot asks jealously, "What was she doing here? What was she saying to you?" Miss LossDream says, "I was here to ask him if he remembered anything. I told him I still loved him and that he has to fight for us and fight to remember. I explained to him that only once he remembers, we can get back our true lives together and he'd be happy again." Simons says, "And you Miss DreamNot knew that if Miss LossDream kept raising the issue, Principal Toombs would begin to remember. What you didn't know is he was remembering. I saw him crying when he smashed his new hand held computer chip sized computer. The night my dream came true and was performed in front of all of Dreamville he related to the story and he remembered even more. I know. I saw his genuine tears of pain." Principal Toombs says, "Simon confronted me about my crying and instead of letting him help me I lashed out in anger. For the past ten years that's the only emotion I've known a part from the pain from being dreamless because of you." Simon says, "And this caused him to push away Miss LossDream and be without his true love by his side." Miss DreamNot says, "That's not true. All these years his true love was by his side." Simon says, "That's right, in your own mind, you were, weren't you Miss DreamNot." Principal Toombs says, "I remember you developed this imaginary relationship in your head." Simon says, "You cleverly implemented yourself as Principal Toombs secretary allowing you to know everything about him, his itinerary, who he had appointments to see, which teachers he had to advise, which students he had to discipline and even when and what he ate so when, out of the blue, he started frequenting Miss LossDream's classroom you were infuriated. Furious, you initiated your ultimate plan." Miss DreamNot says, "Lies, lies. You're all in cahoots, conspiring against me." Simon says, "Well yes we are because you want to rule Dreamville with evil intentions and we want to restore the ancient Dreamville royal monarchy but first tell us how you plan to be queen again." Miss DreamNot says, "Simple, so simple yet even the dream squad cops can't catch me and no one believes any of you. You're right about what I did ten years ago and now I simply have been spreading the outsider's dirt everywhere rendering all Dreamvillians dreamless, unhappy and without their precious technology. They're all at my mercy making me the official queen. BOW BEFORE YOUR QUEEN." She pushes Jilla into Almont's arms and points the shot gun at all of them as they huddle in a group. She's about to pull the trigger when she gets jumped from behind and shoots straight into the ceiling making a giant hole in both the ceiling and Principal Toombs bedroom floor. She drops the shot gun on the floor.

125

She's pinned face forward against the floor by Rino who ran all the way from his house. Simon helps Rino pin her down with his knees on her back. Principal Toombs takes her shotgun away from her and places it behind the whole group, out of her sight. Rino says, "Sorry it took me so long to get here." Simon says, "You don't need to apologize." Jilla says, "Yeah Rino, it's not like you knew where we were." Rino says, "Oh yeah. Well everyone in Dreamville clearly heard every word she said. What she said is better than any confession." Miss LossDream says, "Listen." "Clip, clop, clippity, clop…. Clip, clop, clippity, clop…" Rino says, "Those are the horses of the dream squad." Simon says, "Hopefully they heard Miss DreamNot's confession." Rino says, "If not the dream squad chief has the evidence to banish her from Dreamville." Miss DreamNot says, "I'm your queen." She overpowers the two boys as she gets up, pushes them off of her and pushes towards the rest of the group. She screams, "BOW BEFORE YOUR QUEEN. ALL OF YOU BOW BEFORE ME." Principal Toombs starts to glow brightly and says, "NEVER. YOU WILL NEVER BE QUEEN. YOU HAVE EVIL IN YOUR HEART THAT MAKES YOU MORE COMMON THAN A COMMON DREAMER." Miss DreamNot arches over in pain as he says these words. She tumbles to her knees with agony on her face but no one pities her. None of them reach out to her. Miss LossDream begins to glow too and says, "Miss DreamNot I hate to see you suffer. Look in your heart and you will see there has always been another who loved you and with time you could easily love him." Miss DreamNot crawls along the floor but none of them notice where she's crawling. She wraps her fingers around the shotgun and quickly stands up pointing at them once again. Miss DreamNot laughs, "Ha-ha. Ha-ha. Aha. You think you've won but you haven't. I've only just begun. Principal Toombs walks towards her. Miss LossDream says, "No." Principal Toombs keeps walking forwards until the barrel of the gun is right against his chest. He says, "Shoot me Miss DreamNot and then shoot you yourself. End it all. End the ancient royal family of Dreamville." She clicks the shotgun and Principal Toombs doesn't flinch. Principal Toombs keeps walking forward and has Miss DreamNot pressed against the golden door. Principal Toombs says, "I knew you didn't have it in you to shoot anyone." Suddenly the door begins to shake, sparks fly everywhere, the room begins to shake, the house begins to shake, the hill begins to shake, the town of Dreamville begins to shake and the dream squad cops fall off of the startled stallions. The door opens as a bright blinding but astonishingly beautiful white light fills the room, the house, the hill, the whole town of Dreamville.

Outside of Principal Toombs house, light is everywhere in Dreamville, as the Dreamvillians immerge from their houses and stare at the Principal Toombs hill and house. The houses are fading back to the color of white. The fences are fading back to white, and the Dreamvillians cheer, "Yahoo… Yahoo… Yahoo…" Everywhere they cheer. They watch as the black dust is lifted from the Dreamville soil and is sucked up the hill into Principal Toombs house. Mrs. LandDream yells, "The Trees are coming back to life." Mr. DreamsAlot yells, "The plants are coming back to life." Mrs. Alldream yells, "The flowers are coming back to life." Mrs. Dreamlee yells, "The crops are coming back to life." Mrs. DreamScifi yells, "The vegetable gardens are coming back to life." Mayor Alldream yells, "The fruit orchards are coming back to life." Mr. Dreamlee yells, "Everything's coming back to life." They cheer and rejoice as the technologies start functioning again. They cheer louder when their hand held computer chip sized computers start functioning again too.

Inside Principal Toombs house, Jilla, Almont, Rino, Miss LossDream, Principal Toombs, Miss DreamNot and Simon observe in amazement as the door sucks all the black dust until there was none left to suck. The light dims but the door does not shut. They all look inside from a distance. Jilla says, "I wonder why it's staying open." The light envelopes Principal Toombs and changes him into a clean, healthy, handsome, black haired, well-clothed Kingly looking gentlemen with a crown encrusted with diamonds on his head. Suddenly, the light surrounds Miss LossDream turning her into the same beautiful woman with auburn hair and sparkly green eyes but with a golden velvet dress fit for a queen. The furniture becomes new and glistening with red velvets, golden legs and glass top tables. The kitchen is brand new with sparkling new stainless steel appliances, plates of gold and silverware of silver and a table with chairs fit for a feast with royals. The windows are stripped of the black paint and the walls are white. Everywhere they look the house is transformed into an estate for a royal family with a grand white staircase to the upstairs. The walls are repaired and the ceiling is repaired. They look out the windows and see the grass coming to life, the plants coming to life, the flowers coming to life, the orchard coming to life and the gargoyles are glistening and golden as they shine in the sunlight. They all look at the door that still isn't closed. Almont says, "What more will it do?" Principal Toombs says, "There isn't anything else I would ask the door to do." Miss LossDream says, "I have one request from the door. Please bring the dream squad chief to Miss DreamNot." Once she finishes her request, the door shakes, sparks and starts moving forwards towards Miss DreamNot. Miss DreamNot shoots at the open door. "Caboum… Caboum… Caboum…" The door chases her all around the room. Suddenly, the dream squad chief walks out of the door. Confused he looks at Miss DreamNot but before he can say anything she shoots him. "Caboum…" They all watch him fall to the floor, dead. Miss LossDream and Jilla gasps. The door sucks the dream squad chief back inside its frame and keeps chasing Miss DreamNot around the media room until finally the door sucks her in too, closes and implodes leaving behind sparkles floating through the air. Almont's virtualcast starts to broadcast and the media clown says, "Everything becomes serene and tranquil as this Sunday's events come to a positively dreamy close."

He quickly turns it off and says, "Uh… Sorry about that." They all pull out their hand held computer sized personal computers and see that they function properly. Everything's functioning properly. Jilla asks, "What happened to Miss DreamNot?" Rino says, "Jilla bow." She turns around and sees everyone in the room bowing before Principal Toombs and Miss LossDream. Principal Toombs says, "Please rise and stand my fellow Dreamvillians. There's no need to bow to me. I may have gained my royal name back but I'm still Principal Toombs." They all stand up straight and Jilla walks up to Miss LossDream and she hugs her. Jilla's stomach rumbles and she says, "Oh my… Sorry, I'm a little hungry." Rino pulls the chocolate bars out of his pocket and says, "Here Jilla." Jilla hugs Rino and says, "Thank you I'll break a piece off for everyone here. They all enjoy a piece of chocolate. Simon asks, "Principal Toombs what is your real name?" Principal Toombs replies, "My name's Régimand DreamRoyal the tenth and Miss DreamNot's really Amérie DreamRoyal Alldream. Unfortunately, she has been banished from Dreamville but fortunately she's banished with the man who loves her." Simon asks, "Who's the man who loves her?" Miss LossDream replies, "The dream squad chief has always loved her." Simon says, "That's why he was so reluctant to help us catch her and have her banished." Jilla asks, "But how? We all saw him get killed." King Régimand DreamRoyal says, "Indeed, he's not dead and yes he didn't want her banned so he turned a blind eye to everything illegal that she was doing but now they can both freely live in the shack in the forbidden wall. They'll be happy. At least, he'll be happy." King Régimand DreamRoyal opens his brand new golden front door and says let's rejoice in the new summer festival." They all walk outside and are in awe at how beautiful the once dead, scary, creepy and decrepit yard and house now sparkles, shines and brightens the whole town of Dreamville. Simon says, "Now we know why his house's the only house on a hill." Almont says, "Look at the golden gargoyles. They're smiling at us." King Régimand DreamRoyal says, "Legend once explained that these gargoyles come alive at night and guard the outskirts of Dreamville from being invaded by outsiders. I don't think it's really true but a great dreamed up story." They walk down the hill as the dream squad's cops arrive with their temporarily appointed dream squad chief, Simon tells them, "Collect the tape recorder and the taped confession. You'll find it under the table, under the only open window in the media room." One dream squad cop replies, "Sure thing Mr. Simon Dreamlee." Almont says, "Look at that everyone!" Almont points at the forbidden forest wall and Jilla says, "See the forest animals frolicking in the Deamville fields." Simon says, "Everything's happening so fast. How's this possible?" Rino says, "As a man of science, I have to admit that there's a lot of magic even in Dreamville that can't be explained." They reach the bottom of the steep hill covered in Apple orchard trees, grape vines, wild lilies, wild sunflowers, wild tulips, wild blue bells and coco plants. Mrs. Dreamlee yells, "Simon, oh Simon. Come here." His parents run up to him and his father raises him onto his shoulders. Mr. Dreamlee says, "My hero is my boy." Jilla's parents yell, "Jilla, sweetheart." They run up to her and hug her. Rino's father yells, "Rino DreamScifi, you really are… Oh come here and give us a hug." Rino runs up to them and hugs his parents. Mayor Alldream says, "Your Majesty." He bows before his king. King DreamRoyal says, "Please stand." Mayor Alldream stands up and says, "Almont, I'm so happy you're okay." Almont runs to his father and awkwardly shakes his hand. His father pulls him towards him and hugs him. King Régimand says, "Let's walk through the streets and celebrate at the summer festivities!" He takes Miss LossDream's hand and they walk hand in hand. They walk through the streets of Dreamville behind King Régimand DreamRoyal as he waves at his loyal subjects. They bow as he walks by and he begins to sing angelically.

Dream, dream, dream,
My citizens, Dreamvillians,
Dream,
You're my acquaintances,
My friends,
And my family,

I'm the true descendant
Of the ancient DreamRoyals
But please
Don't bow to me,
Stand and rise
And sing with me.
Dream, dream, dream,
My fellow Dreamvillians,
Dream,
Dream about,
Anything, everything, something,
And share your happiness with all of us.
Dream, dream, dream,
My friends,
Keep on dreaming
And Keep
Dreams coming true,
Dream, dream, dream,
Dreams do come
True.

The Dreamvillians begin to stand, rise, smile and sing along with their loveable king. They follow him all the way to the summer festival outdoor room. They sing and feast all weekend long without going home to sleep and dream. On Sunday evening, during the last hours of the summer celebration, they, the musically inclined dreamers, even organize a quick re-perform of the performance of Simon's latest dream come true depicting the saga of King Régimand DreamRoyal, Miss LossDream and Amérie DreamRoyal Alldream from ten years ago. Afterwards, King DreamRoyal says, "So Simon, I guess you'll be dreaming up the sequel some time now." Simon says, "No need, I've lived through the sequel." Mrs. Dreamlee says, "Oh he will. He'll dream the sequel and produce it too." King DreamRoyal says, "I can't wait to watch it." Simon says, "After the last week's events, it won't be for awhile because I think I'll filter out my dreams and just enjoy this truly happy ending." They all joyously laugh, "Ha-ha… Hi…Hi…. Aha… Ha-ha…"

Late that same Sunday night, silently soaking in their renewed Dreamville, the new surroundings romanticizing everyone's senses, Simon and his parents start walking home in the bright moonlight from the summer festivities. They walk up the streets and the drives. They walk up their driveway and into their house. Once inside, Simon turns to his parents and says, "Sweet dreams mom and dad. I'm going to bed." His parents follow him upstairs and say, "Sweet dreams son. They go into their bedrooms. Simon walks to his bed and decides to go in the attic and observe everyone going happily home to once again dream and have their dreams come true. He observes all his neighbors enter their houses, their light go out and he hears the silence of the night fill the once again calm, serene, dreamy streets, drives and roads of Dreamville. But he's suddenly startled by a rather large rustling sound as he peers into the night sky to see one of King DreamRoyal's golden gargoyles flapping his wings and flying in front of the moon. He quickly looks at the kingly hill and sees all the gargoyles walking and flying around. Simon says, "Well I'll be, the legend's true. They do wake and protect us during the night." All of a sudden, the original gargoyle that he observed flying high in the sky is looking back at him from the end of his telescope. The wings of the large mythical creature make a light breeze that rustles Simon's hair. Simon says, "Hello. I'm Simon Dreamlee." The gargoyle says, "Hello Simon Dreamlee. I'm Gargantua and I'm here to protect you." Simon says, "Protect me? You mean King DreamRoyal." Gargantua says, "You as well being that you're the king's closest friend and the truth dreamer. You see we gargoyles are indebted to King DreamRoyal's family for the past couple centuries because they risked their lives to save us from extinction at the hands of the outsiders. After learning that we come alive at night they feared us instead of getting to know us. The outsiders automatically don't like what they don't understand. His ancestors watched through their looking window as the outsiders came after us and tried to kill us all by smashing us to bits during the daylight hours. The DreamRoyals came out of their sanctuary of Dreamville even though they could have been killed themselves. They waited in the woods for us to wake up and when we did they tried to reason with us but we wouldn't listen so they kidnapped us and brought us here. We were angry at first but then they showed us what had happened to our relatives and we wept. They granted us refuge here for as long as we wanted to stay and we decided to stay forever and be Dreamville's night time guardians." Simon smiles, "There must be so much more to this fascinating story. Your story's legendary and I'm so happy to have the privilege of learning that... You're completely truly alive at night and really are protecting us. I can't wait to tell everyone." Gargantua replies, "Now you're not supposed to know that we come alive at night so I'm sorry to do this but…" The gargoyle blows some golden dust in Simon's face and Simon gets drowsy. Gargantua flies inside his house and carries him to his bedroom. Simon struggles to stay awake as he tries to see through his blurred vision. Once Gargantua places him into his bed, he attaches Simon's dream catcher to Simon's head. Simon's dog, Boomboom Booya, jumps on his bed to sleep at his feet and his cat, Frankie Noodles, jumps into her cat bed to sleep. Simon's head rests on his pillow and as you all know, he instantly closes his eyes and falls to sleep. He starts to dream. Gargantua observes the smile on Simon's face as he sleeps soundly. Gargantua says, "Don't worry little truth dreamer you're well protected while you dream in your sleep." Gargantua walks quietly out of Simon's bedroom and closes the door behind him, he walks up to the attic, flies out the window and into the night sky to join his fellow gargoyle night guardians.

Chapter Fifteen – Fairytale Monday

Simon Dreamlee wakes up from his long needed restful sleep on Monday morning. He's surprised to find his dream catcher attached to his head, that he's covered in some kind of gold dust and that he's in his bed. He detaches his dream catcher form his head as he stretches his limbs. He yawns and pets his dog, Boomboom Booya. When he sits up, his cat, Frankie Noodles, purrs and jumps on his lap. The birds are chirping outside and the cloudless sky, full of sunshine greets his smiling face. Everything, truly now is back to normal. He opens his bedroom door and runs up to the attic to look through his telescope at the king's castle. Now that they live together, he sees him walking to his hover car with Miss LossDream. They get inside and start hovering down the apple orchard filled hill and towards Dreamtrue School. Simon watches as people let their cats out for their daily ventures and let their birds spread their wings. People walk along the streets with their dogs on leashes and wave at one and other as they pass each other on the sidewalks. Simon says, "It's a happy Monday, a normal dreamy Dreamville Monday."

Simon runs downstairs from the attic to his bedroom and puts his hand held computer chip sized computer and his virtual communicator in his pocket. He's ready to go to school. He runs downstairs to the kitchen where he finds his father listening to the virtualcast with the media clowns commentary. Mr. Dreamlee turns to his son and says, "Happy Monday son!" Simon replies, "Happy Monday dad." Mrs. Dreamlee enters the kitchen humming and stops to say, "Happy morning my most lovely dreamy family." Simon says, "Happy Monday mom." Mr. Dreamlee says, "Happy Monday dear." They all smile at each other. Simon's mom walks to the fridge, takes out some blueberry and maple syrup. She says, "I'll make pancakes from the fresh ground flower. They'll be very yummy!" Simon says, "That sounds great mom but I'll just have some of these fresh cherries on my way to school. Bye." Simon's parents both say, "Bye

Simon." Simon opens the backdoor and closes it behind him. He takes a few moments to smell the fresh air. He walks to his hover bike and starts hovering down his driveway. He hovers at the end of the driveway looking up at the king's castle. His new fascination is the gargoyles. Simon says, "I wonder if that legends true." Simon has no recollection of the night before and meeting Gargantua. The golden dust not only made him drowsy but erased his memory of their meeting. He shakes his head and says, "I feel like I already know the answer but I'm not sure how I know." He turns right and hovers to the intersection to meet up with Almont. Almont says, "Happy Monday Simon." Simon says, "Happy Monday indeed" They hover towards Dreamtrue School. Everything's back to normal in Dreamville as they hover by their neighbors. Mrs. Dreammore and Mrs. LandDream say, "Congratulations Simon. I can't wait to see your next dream in theatres." Simon replies, "Thank you, thank you." Mr. BottomDream says, "Good job chap. Keep your dreams coming true and ours too." Simon replies, "Thanks Mr. BottomDream." Simon and Almont smile at each other as they hover on their way to Dreamtrue School. They get to school and park their hover bikes in the hover bike parkade and walk towards the front door. Almont asks, "I wonder who our new principal will be?" Simon replies, "I think that you'll be pleasantly surprised." They reach the front door and Almont says, "King DreamRoyal why are you here? Oh pardon me." Almont bows to him. King DreamRoyal replies, "You don't have to bow to me Almont. Please stand up. I want to be a regular Dreamville citizen such as you so I kept my post here as the principal. You may all address me as Principal DreamRoyal." Almont stands up and looks at Simon and then at Principal DreamRoyal. Almont asks, "But why when you could have everything done for you as you command?" Principal DreamRoyal says, "Almont that's a great question and here's my answer. You're late for class so you better get going before I have to punish the two of you." King DreamRoyal winks at Simon and Almont says, "Sir, yes sir. Quick Simon let's get to class." Simon winks back at King DreamRoyal and says, "Good one Régimand, good one!" Simon and Almont enter their school and run down the now warm inviting golden hued hall to their musically inclined dreamer's classroom. They enter their classroom and walk to their seats. Miss LossDream enters the classroom, stands in front of the class and says, "Happy Monday everyone. I trust everyone has a dream to share today." She walks to her desk and says, "Let's all enjoy Simon's Dream shall we." Simon places his computer chip sized hand held computer in the pod on his desktop and presses play. His dream materializes on the big screen for all to watch. Simon hadn't taken the time to review his dream and is looking forward to being as mesmerized by his dream just like his classmates.

His dream starts with the little boy who represents hope dancing freely on the stage with the key around his neck. The music he created in his dream is fun, happy and brilliantly suited to the happy ending. The cackle on the evil woman fades and disappears altogether. The light on the stage becomes brighter as the golden door appears, opens and sucks and raises the broken heart of the man's true love and mends it back together. The black dust is sucked into the door and all the plants come back to life. Suddenly the male dancer comes on stage wrapped in the black cloth. He twirls around as the black cloth unravels and is also sucked into the golden door. He dances freely on the stage and into the arms of his true love as she now enters the stage. She picks up her floating heart and hands it over to her true love and they embrace. The evil woman dances awkwardly and pitifully on the stage and is sucked into the door. The door shuts and the curtain is drawn. The two true lovers are in front of the curtain still in their embrace as crowns materialized on their heads. The little boy dances around them and holds up the key for everyone to read. He sings the inscription out loud, "Truth is stronger than evil." The lights go out and the saga is complete but suddenly, a golden gargoyles face appears through the darkness and sings, "Dreamville and the DreamRoyals are well protected at night truth dreamer." The song plays beautifully, happily and joyously as the sequel ends positively.

Truth dreamer I am,
I dreamt a dream of an event from ten years ago,
I brought you hope that peace will be restored,
Because I believe that truth
Is always be stronger than evil.
The golden door awaken by ancient royal,
The man and woman,
Truly love and reunite in their passionate
Embrace,
Banished the evil woman forever from Dreamville,
But do not fear this evil woman has a man who loves her
And will be with her to live out their days
In the outside world,
Living in the forbidden forest wall

Truth dreamer I am,
I dreamt a dream of an event from ten years ago,
I brought you hope that peace will be restored,
Because I believe that truth
Will always be stronger than evil.
She will never return.
This ancient royal's cool,
Deservingly he dreams once again.
Enduring ten years of having his dreams stolen from him
He demands that no one bow to him and treat him like everyone else in
His beloved town of Dreamville
Where dreams do indeed come
True.
They come true!

Principal and King DreamRoyal walks in the class as Simon's dream ends. King DreamRoyal takes Miss Loss Dream's left hand with his left hand while he gets down on one knee and asks, "Cédrina will you be my wife and my queen." Miss LossDream replies, "Yes Régimand." He slips a golden diamond ring on her left hand ring finger and takes Miss LossDream by her waist and kisses her in front of the class. Jilla sighs as do all the other girls who begin to stream them on the internet with their virtual communicators. All of Dreamville cheers and the media clowns say, "Everything's dreamy in Dreamville as the sun shines, the flowers send their perfume in the air and King DreamRoyal proposes to and kisses his true love, Miss Cédrina LossDream. She dreamily accepts the ring. Sigh." Jilla says, "Oh how romantic." All the girls say, "So dreamily romantic." Simon covers his eyes with his hands as do all the other boys. Almont says, "You had to dream about a love story." Simon says, "Let me know when it's safe to look again." Everyone in Dreamville laughs happily, wholesomely and of course dreamily.

The End

<u>Epilogue</u>

Simon Dreamlee sleeps soundly every night dreaming up his dreamily fantastic songs for the next year without a hint of clues just simple songs for fun, dancing, singing and enjoying. He celebrated his thirteenth birthday with Almont Alldream, Jilla MusiDream, Booya, Frankie Noodles, Rino DreamScifi, King Régimand DreamRoyal the tenth, Miss LossDream and Wendy the cow. They had a great time celebrating with chocolate cake, vanilla ice cream and fluffy, yummy, dream whip. Dreamville celebrated with them as well at one of the dreamy dream filled summer festivities and all its glorious music by the musically inclined dreamers.

One dreamy evening before the sunset, Simon stares through his telescope at the DreamRoyals castle and hill when he notices the golden gargoyle statues seem to be looking at him. He seems to remember they were all looking at the castle the last night he laid eyes on those stone statues. Simon begins to document any sudden changes in the appearance of the gargoyles on any night he's free to look through his telescope. In a year's time, Simon compiles, documents and dates the days where there are significant changes in the statues appearances even though it's slight, miniscule and unbelievable, Simon chooses to say nothing to anyone, not even to his best dreamy friend Almont about his observations, Simon's happy keeping this secret all to himself for now.

Just before the year is up, Simon releases his hit song titled "The Gargoyles". Every Dreamvillian and Outsider loves the dreamy song and plays it over and over.

Rocking with the Gargoyles
All day and night long
Rocking Gargoyles
Rock, Rock, Rock

Rocking along with the Gargoyles
All noon and evening
Rocking Gargoyles
Rock, Rock, Rock

Rapping with the Gargoyles
All day and night long
Rapping with the Gargoyles
Rap, Rap, Rap

Rapping with the Gargoyles
All noon and evening
Rapping Gargoyles
Rap, Rap, Rap

Hip hopping with the Gargoyles
All day and night long
Hip hopping Gargoyles
Hip, Hip, Hip

Hip hopping with the Gargoyles
All noon and evening
Hip hopping Gargoyles
Hip, Hip, Hip

All is well, good, wholesome and dreamy in Dreamville and its dream inclined citizens and especially for Simon Dreamlee and his new dreamy fascination with these unknown stone statues and the myth that surround their very existence in Dreamville and with Miss DreamNot's banishment there's no need to worry. Simon says, "Worrying is not very Dreamvillian like." He gazes at the stars as he dreamily lives his Dreamvillian life.

Author Bio

R. E. Brémaud earned her bachelor of arts degree from the University of Manitoba with a major in English literature and three minors in French literature, history, and psychology. She resides in Manitoba, Canada. This is her first book.